B F Dealeo

FIFTY SHADES
of BRAINS

B F Dealeo is a pen name used by two Seattle-based writers who met while studying literature at the University of Washington. One is a father, video gamer, and comics geek. The other has sense enough not to give out any personal information. Between them they have written, co-written, and edited thirteen books plus hundreds of articles and book reviews.

This is their first novel.

BOOKS BY B F DEALEO

(A few. But we're not telling.)

FIFTY SHADES
of BRAINS

FIFTY SHADES
of BRAINS

B F Dealeo

Ambauminable, LLC | Seattle

ISBN: 978-1-937914-02-8 (trade)
978-1-937914-03-5 (ebook)

The CIP Data is out there.
Go ahead and catalog this yourself, though.
It's kinda fun, and nobody likes a copycat.

Thanks to our amazing cover model, Kathy Lindenmayer.
(image used with permission)

www.fiftyshadesofbrains.com

Printed in the United States of America
number number number number arbitrary number

For E L James,

the master of the publishing universe.

We had a great time with your book.

We're hoping you'll get a kick out of ours.

ACKNOWLEDGEMENTS

Thanks to all of our early readers: Rob H, Snow W, Lara S, Kathleen S, Karla A, Mike D, Diane M, Renate (there's only one), Dan F, Dawn R, and Marin Y. Appreciation to Bill B and Richard G for help with the cover. And everyone else who gave us feedback on the idea, good and bad, including blank faced stares and conspiratorial giggles, you have our gratitude.

A nod to my wife, who still refuses to read it. Ditto for my partner-in-crime's soon-to-be mortified family.

Finally, a tip of the hat to Professor William Dunlop, all covered in chalk, the best English teacher ever.

FIFTY SHADES
of BRAINS

CHAPTER ONE

I scowl in frustration at the cars that fill the intersection. Flipped over, crashed into each other or into telephone poles or through storefronts. It's your classic post-apocalyptic scene. Yawning car doors, broken or missing side mirrors. Bodies slumped over wheels. Some with heads, some without. And of course all the windows are shattered or boarded up. *How is a girl supposed to check her damned hair?*

I make do with a small mirror shard that I find poking out of a mound of trash next to a toppled fire hydrant. No water, of course. Also, no firemen. I heave a heavy sigh.

I squint into the mirror and sigh again. My hair still has a life of its own. Luckily for me, none of the corpses do.

"Huuuuuuugggggghhhrrrrrr." *I spoke too soon.*

There's a roamer in a black SUV in front of me. It paws the door open and stands up awkwardly. It's completely uncoordinated. *I can so relate!* If it comes for me, at least it's going to be slow. And probably solo. Inside the wall, it's unlikely the thing has any undead friends nearby. I desperately push some stray hairs behind my ears and get ready to race off.

"Glllllllluuuuuuuuk." *Did it just make a duck sound?* I pause and look at the thing a bit more closely. It clears its throat and spits something green into the street. *Is that a tooth?*

"Water?" it asks, stumbling toward me. It's human, I realize -- a guy sleeping rough despite the glut of free housing. I don't have time for this. *I'm late.*

"Try the shelter," I shout, lifting Velma, my push scooter, over some rubble. I start kicking down the street, neatly steering around the wreckage and the bum, leaving him staring dumbly at my slowly disappearing back.

If I don't hurry I'm going to miss this interview!

My roommate, Penelope, chose today of all days to get sick. She didn't get bit, though, so it's not the virus. As far as I can tell, it's a combo of drinking too much and yet another bad piece of meat. Literally, that is.

Power is spotty so food -- especially highly prized bits of fresh mystery meat -- tends to spoil fast.

"You and your barter system," I told her, tucking a ragged blanket around her shapely body just that morning. "If you're going to give it up, at least give it up for a decent piece of meat."

Penelope gave me a look.

"You know what I mean," I told her, rolling my eyes.

"I'm just trying to survive," she rasped, wiping at her mouth. "If it's you or him, and you've treated him right once upon a time, he may save you. Or even come for you when the zombies swarm. Sex is the new friending, Ro. I'm rebuilding the community."

Even with puke on her lip she was hotter than me.

"Yes, but you shouldn't give it away for a bad squirrel burger," I chided.

"I didn't. He gave us breakfast, too." She grinned and shook a cereal box, and we both dug in.

Well, she dug in. I only had a couple of nibbles. Any more and I would have popped the zipper on the sexy ensemble she'd assembled for me for my big interview with the man everyone's heard of but few have seen. I wasn't even sure if I'd ever seen a decent photo of Green. With no internet or TV, nobody really knows what's going on anymore. Although the newsletters do their best to keep everybody informed about nesting hordes and who's sleeping with the ruling counsel and all that.

I did know Green was extraordinarily rich and überpowerful and that he would be speaking at Survival School graduation. Penelope -- ever pushy -- somehow managed to finagle an interview with him so she could write about him in the school newsletter. Gas, coffee, and booze were almost impossible to come by, but all those abandoned offices had Xerox machines and reams of paper galore. I swear even the zombies put out their own 'zine.

* * *

I arrive at his fifty-story building in downtown Seattle with minutes to spare, despite the ten grueling minutes I spent behind a gigantic cargo bike loaded with organic kimchee. Seattle's dream of becoming the local food capital of the world has finally come true. Unfortunately, there are only a few thousand people left in the city to enjoy it. As much as you can enjoy a hyper local meal when you're more than likely to become one yourself.

Damn zombies. They're such a buzz kill.

I toss my hair out of my eyes and stare up at Green's massive tower. It's beautiful. More than that, it's completely intact.

Holy cow. How did he manage to salvage all those mirrored windows? And keep them so clean?

I look up and see a tiny white figure high above the street; he appears to be washing the windows. Rumor has it it's the one building in the city where everything works: water, electricity, even the freaking toilets. I swallow hard, suddenly nervous.

Oh Penelope, how could you do this to me? Who am I to interview the most powerful man in all of Seattle? The man who has everything anyone could ever want, the man who keeps all of us safe?

Buck up, my inner drill sergeant yells at me. *Now drop and give me twenty!*

The entire first floor is empty except for a central desk. It's all sandstone and glass and steel and space. The immaculate woman there has impossibly fine, white-blonde hair and eyes that are barely blue. She's clean and dressed impeccably. Her manners are impeccable, too. She doesn't even seem to register the latex-and-heels ensemble Pen poured me into. I wonder if she can tell I'm not wearing any underwear.

"I'm here to see Mr. Green. Aurora Foyle for Penelope Spunk."

"Please sign here." I sign a clipboard and she hands me a visitor badge. It's spattered with something brown. Ketchup? I wonder, sniffing at it.

I smell copper. *Holy crap. It's dried blood!*

"Mr. Green's office is one floor down from the penthouse."

I nod and head toward the stairs.

She interrupts me politely. "You're welcome to use one of the elevators. They're fully operational."

I blush. Of course they are. I walk past the two pale, muscle-bound security guards in well-cut uniforms. One's wearing Doc Martens. The other's wearing sandals and socks. Not even a zombie apocalypse could kill that bad fashion statement. I shake my head and walk by. They stare straight ahead and don't even notice my curves.

Hmmm, maybe not everything in the building is fully operational.

The walls inside the elevator are mirrored just like the outside of the building. I push a button then bite my lip, realizing now that my hair looks awful from every angle. In fact, I look like I just crawled out of a greasy grave. Since Penelope and I live in a basement apartment next door to an old auto repair place, I practically did.

I desperately swat at my hair, then try to tuck my boobs into my jacket. They bounce right back out and up toward my face. My black rubber jacket's zipper is stuck at nipple level. I give up and pick at the blood on my badge.

The doors open and there's another lobby and another woman, dressed just like the one on the first floor. And she's got the same coloring. Pale guards, pale receptionists. I roll my eyes.

Albinos? Really? What is this, a Dan Brown novel?

Just then another woman appears carrying a glass of iced water, which she offers to me like it's the most natural thing in the world. I take the glass and just stare at it for a moment, watching the ice bob in the cold, clear liquid. She gestures me toward a chair near the tall glass windows.

I gape at her for a moment. *They* do *have continuous power here.* Then I sit, trying to still my fluttering heartbeat. *Get a grip, Foyle.*

"Mr. Green will be with you in a moment. May I take your jacket?" one of the albino Barbies asks me.

"Um, that's okay," I say. "I, uh, I don't have anything on underneath."

She nods like that's perfectly normal and struts off in a pair in heels you could impale somebody with.

I take a slow delicious sip of ice water, the first time I've had anything but tepid, boiled water in months, and stare out the glass-walls at the city.

Maybe it's my mood or the early morning hour, but I suddenly feel like narrating a brief history of the zombie apocalypse and how it's impacted our city the last seven years.

Below me, the streets are clogged with cars, although in some places they've been pushed aside so what passes for traffic can still get through. Most of the cars have been stripped by the scavenger crews. They look a little like the desiccated bodies you still see in the sketchier neighborhoods.

Like mine. My neighborhood, not my body.

Ahead of me is Elliott Bay, littered with capsized ferries and half-sunk tanker ships. Water is a natural barrier against the dead and lucky for us, Seattle's practically surrounded by it. Zombies can't swim and those that try to cross via the sea floor or river bottom or whatever you want to call it usually fall apart before they get to the other side.

To the north I see Queen Anne Hill. On the other side of it is the canal, our northern border, which runs from Puget Sound to Lake Washington. All of the bridges are blocked and guarded now; the neighborhoods on the other side are lost to the hordes. I can't see them, but there are crops growing in what used to be the Seattle Center and along the waterfront. The gardens, organized by Green, provide the city's inhabitants with fruits and veggies. The inhabitants, in turn, provide the gardens with fertilizer. Which is better than using dead bodies, I guess.

Either way -- ew.

To the south, I see a few wind turbines and green patches on top of apartment buildings. Further off, I see the old sports stadiums, now giant warehouses full of scavenged food, emergency water, batteries, bullets, etc. The wall is just south of the stadiums. It's been thrown together bit by bit over the last few years. It's mostly piled up blocks of broken concrete, toppled cranes, shipping containers and cars, with some chain link and whatever else the crews have been able to drag there. The wall stretches from the southern tip of Elliott Bay to Lake Washington along the I-90 corridor.

I-90 itself is completely clogged with traffic, as is every other major freeway, highway, thoroughfare and bike trail. Seattle still has a traffic problem that nobody wants to deal with.

We also have neighborhoods that nobody wants to deal with. West Seattle, Ballard, Fremont and U District and the Eastside are all on the wrong side of the water and infested with the undead. But our city is ever-expanding. Or at least that's the idea. Rumor has it Green is currently trying to reclaim a few nearby islands, like Vashon. That is if the handful of surviving yurt-dwellers there will have it. They're sort of a militant bunch.

I stare south, trying to see Pioneer Square, where Penelope and I live and attend Survival School. I work there, too. It's nerve-wracking living less than a mile from the wall and the zombie hordes on the other side. But every day, the wall is inspected and reinforced with whatever we can use. We all pull shifts there, even students. These days, it's all about keeping safe.

Keeping safe and staying alive. Or, when that doesn't work, at least staying dead once you do die.

I look down at my water and notice my reflection. My hair's come undone yet again. *Ugh.*

One of the albino Barbies is suddenly at my elbow. "Mr. Green will see you now."

"Oh!" I startle, nearly spilling the water. I gulp down the rest of the icy deliciousness and follow her to a set of gigantic double doors. As I approach, I hear something behind the doors, something familiar.

I close my eyes, grasp the handle and pull.

"Huuuuuuugggggghhhrrrrrr!"

It's the classic zombie rasp I've heard imitated over and over again at school. I turn and see a trim man shutting a door, cutting off the sound. I stare at his tight ass as I step forward.

Oh my.

Then I promptly trip and fall face first into the office. *Holy shit.*

I am on my hands and knees and suddenly there's a pair of perfectly groomed bare feet in front of me. I scramble upright. The feet belong to a tall, muscular man whose hair is wonderfully unruly, like he has a supply of hair gel. He's wearing a white track suit. He was the one closing the door where the sound came from.

"Miss Foyle." He extends a long-fingered hand. I realize with a start it's not his.

"I'm Caligula Green," he says, nodding to the hand, neatly severed just above the wrist. "And please accept my apologies for this. It's a little souvenir that somehow got out of place."

He looks at it with bemusement then sets it down on a tastefully-lit pedestal. I notice a brass plaque on the pedestal. "First Kill," it reads.

"Of course you will," he says. "Just as I use m skills to the best of *my* ability."

"To help others survive?"

"Yes," he says after a brief pause.

I start to wonder if the rumors are true. Maybe Green really is working on trying to find a cure for this whole zombie thing.

"You, uh, you have a lot of nice stuff," I say, looking around. "The nicest."

"I deserve all of it," he says, leaning back. "I've worked hard for it. Killed for it. And nearly been killed a thousand times. Every day is Black Friday beyond the wall."

He smiles that bemused smile again and my inner smart ass blows a raspberry. The guy is full of himself. *I'd love to be full of him, too, though.*

"Are you important, Mr. Green?" I stare at the question again. "Oops, I mean, are you impotent?"

He inhales sharply and his eyes darken, then blaze, then cool, then cut me to the quick with indifference. *Damn you, Penelope Spunk!*

"No," he answers coldly.

"I'm sorry," I say, nodding at the paper. "That was one of Penelope's questions."

I wonder about his answer, though. He hasn't even glanced at my boobs, despite the fact my left nipple has wiggled its way out of the latex jacket. I swear it's like they have a life of their own.

Just then a white head pokes through the doorway and tells Green he has another appointment. I get up, convinced that I'm about to be given the boot, but instead cancels his meeting.

Before it looked gross and desiccated. Now it looks exquisite, like art.

"Are you all right?" he asks and we finally shake hands, for real. A current runs through me and I suddenly feel like I'm being electrocuted. It's hard to let go.

"I'm, uh, I'm fine," I stammer, blushing. "I'm Aurora Foyle. I'm studying survival with Penelope Spunk, who was scheduled to interview you." I explain about Pen's food poisoning and he nods, his eyes hooded.

"Sit." He gestures to a white leather couch.

I look around at the furniture, the carpet, the coffee table. Everything is white, which must be hard to pull off when your job keeps you covered in blood and gore. I stare at him as I take a seat on the couch, which smells delicious. Like candy. Then I realize, it's not the couch, it's him. He not only gorgeous, he's clean. Completely clean. *Probably even down there.*

I'd trade this guy whatever he wanted for a rotten burger, I think, then immediately blush deep red. From the other room, I hear that groaning sound again. Must be some kind of training seminar next door.

When I look up, I see that his eyes are on me. He's watching me intently, but not in the leering way men watch Penelope. I lean forward to pull my roommate's carefully prepared questions and a notebook and pen out of my satchel. He doesn't even seem to notice my boobs spilling out of my impossibly tight top.

"This interview will, uh, appear in the Survival School newsletter," I mumble. My heartbeat speeds up.

"Yes, I know. I'm handing out the degrees at your graduation," he says. "I also designed the curriculum. And convinced the council to build the school five years ago."

He's completely deadpan. *Does that come in handy in his line of work?*

I blush again and stare down at Pen's questions, trying to ignore the sounds from the next room.

Focus, Ro, focus!

"You've killed more zombies than anyone. Why are you still alive?"

I look up at him, my pen poised.

"I know the dead, Miss Foyle," he says matter-of-factly. "How they move, where they'll be, which will attack first if they're in a group. I know when to use an axe, when to use a bullet, and when to simply get out of the way."

The world seems to stop as he leans forward.

"I also know what the dead are drawn to." His eyes are looking me up and down and I blush again. *Maybe I do have a shot.*

I swallow. "Are you just lucky?"

Would you like to get lucky?

He smiles a tight, mysterious smile. "I don't believe in luck, Miss Foyle. I work hard. I make quick decisions. I employ albinos. I also stay in shape, eat right, and use good tools." His eyes are pools of green, like ponds covered in algae.

My inner sex goddess quickly gets a Brazilian wax and puts on a bikini. She's ready to dive right in.

He looks out the window, inviting me to study his profile. "I also control my fear so that I never hesitate."

"Do you enjoy control?"

"No. But in my line of work it pays to be ready. And to understand all my options."

"Do you feel immensely powerful?" *Or do you just look it?*

"I employ forty people. I do my best to keep other 4,000 safe so that they can rebuild what's left of th lives."

He smiles and his teeth gleam. "I feel good abo myself."

Our last tube of toothpaste ran out days ago, an we won't be allocated another for three weeks. I briefl consider using his bathroom in order to stock up on sup plies. *I'd love to get my hands on that hair gel!*

I quickly dismiss the idea and look down at my questions. "Do you answer to the ruling counsel?"

He leans toward me. "I don't answer to anyone, Miss Foyle. I put the undead down and I keep the supplies coming and in return, the counsel gives me whatever I want. Eventually, everyone gives me what I want."

I gasp, then blush, then bite my lip, realizing that I'm blushing. *Breathe, Ro, breathe!* I stare down at Pen's questions, rattled.

"Um, do you do anything besides work?" *Because there are a few things I'd like to do right now.*

"I have varied interests: music, pole vaulting, fifteenth century instruments of torture. Don't we all? But mainly I work. I build things. I help people figure out how to grow food. I reinforce the wall. I make sure we're as saf as we can be. I want to survive."

"Me, too," I whisper and flush again. He leans fo ward, suddenly more interested.

"What are you willing to do to help others s vive?" he asks, his eyes growing impossibly intense.

"Well, I'm ... uh ... I'm about to graduate," I st mer. "I guess I'll use my skills to the best of my ability, everyone's expected to."

The albino Barbie stares at me and raises what would be her eyebrows, if she had eyebrows. *Holy cow. He wants me to stay?*

"I'd like to know about you, Miss Foyle," he says, gesturing me to sit again. "It's only fair."

"There's not much to tell." I flush and immediately, there's that weird moaning sound from the room next door. He leans forward, almost eagerly.

"What are you going to do after you graduate?" He stares at me intently as he rakes his hand through his stunningly unruly hair.

I'm suddenly very warm. *Down there.* "I'll probably get a job in agriculture," I tell him. "Most of my friends are going to be farmers." Except Penelope who wants to become a black market kingpin. Or a cruise director.

"Your gifts would be wasted with all those hoes." His lips curl into a smile. "You should come work with me. Outside the wall. It's quite ... stimulating."

"I'm not sure I'd be able to do that," I mumble. *I'm uncoordinated and unkempt and my body produces pigment.* "I'm sure I'd get bitten."

"Oh, I'd keep you safe."

His voice is dead serious and I believe him. My insides melt a little and my inner child hugs herself and smiles beatifically. *Safe!* "Thanks. I'll, uh, I'll think about it."

"You'd have everything you could ever want."

"You could have anything you want right now," I say, lowering my eyes and looking up at him submissively through my thick auburn lashes. Pen and I have spent hours perfecting that move. But he doesn't even notice. It's like I'm offering him a hammer.

"I'm not interested in sex, Miss Foyle," he says. "I'm only interested in the undead. And I want you to come work with me when I hunt them. You're a talented young woman. I'd love to take advantage of your talents."

Holy fuck. At least he wants me for something. But I need to think about this. I stand up.

"Thank you for the interview, Mr. Green. And the job offer."

"The pleasure has been all mine, Miss Foyle."

CHAPTER TWO

My heart is hammering as I leave the elevator of his building and rush outside. I actually welcome the scent of decay, the putrid breath of the city. It helps me recover from the last few, surreal minutes.

No one has ever looked at me the way Caligula Green looked at me. There was no lust in his eyes, but there was raw unadulterated *something*.

What's his deal?

I made it clear I wanted to be his plaything, but all he seems to want is somebody to reload his shotgun. *And not in a good way.*

And what's with all that stuff about keeping me safe. Wouldn't it be safer to take a farming job than to press my luck as a junior zombie hunter?

Forget it, Ro. Put that all behind you. But the interview continues to eat at me as I head home. Thankfully, it's the only thing.

Penelope and I live in a basement apartment in Pioneer Square, about a half mile from the school. It's dark and dank and still pretty gross. It was once used as storage for the garage next door so there aren't many windows, and the only door is heavily reinforced. I don't mind that we don't have a view. If you can see out, the zombies can get in. Plus, who wants to look at a wasteland?

Pen is sharpening her knives -- literally -- when I walk through the door. The kitchen table is covered with ropes, each one sporting a different knot. In the corner, I see a few tires she's "attacked," covered with cuts and stab marks. She's been studying for finals and looks like she's feeling better.

"You're back! How did it go? What was he like?"

I toss my notebook to her. "Intimidating. Sexy as hell. Dressed all in white. Cold and entirely uninterested in breasts or other body parts." *Any living part, that is. I think back on the severed hand.*

"Who wouldn't want those breasts? Or those lips?" Pen asks, bewildered.

I shrug. "I know, right?"

"Jeez, Ro, maybe he really is impotent. I mean, that's always been the rumor because he's so driven and only seems to think about killing zombies. Most men don't have that kind of focus."

"I know," I say, trying to escape to my room where I can masturbate in peace. But it's impossible to put off Penelope and her persistent questions. I end up telling her about the interview.

"I can't believe you didn't take him up on his job offer," she says when I finish. "You'd have been famous *and* well-fed."

"And dead. Or worse."

I look over at our wind-up alarm clock and realize I'm late for work at the hardware store. My inner time-keeper looks at her wrist then taps her foot impatiently.

"Holy cow! I have to run, Pen. Feel better!"

* * *

Elliott Bay Salvage isn't really a hardware store but that's the closest word that describes the place. Back in the day, it used to be a bookstore, full of creaky wooden stairs, lofts and isolated cubbyholes. Now every corner is full of recycled or reclaimed crap: faucet heads, hammers, dolls, espresso machine parts. There are lots of tools, too, not to mention tools looking for tools and salvaged building materials. We also stock bicycle parts, kitchen supplies, and bits and pieces scrounged from cars: seat belts, suitcases, and personal items pulled from trunks and glove compartments.

Lots of people thought they could outrun the virus. They were wrong.

The store, and others like it, has teams working all over the city and even outside the wall scavenging whatever useful items they can find. Until we start manufacturing things again, we have to make use of every board and nail. Thanks to the zombies, Seattle finally became the recycling paradise it always wanted to be.

We're always busy, mostly with turning away folks who want what we have in stock but don't have the authorization to take it. The council controls all resources. Things were much easier when we used money but then people realized money was pretty worthless. Now you need a ration card or a form signed in triplicate to "buy" anything, even the sad little crayon candles my mother squishes together.

Unless you want to barter, like Pen.

I work at Elliott's a few hours every day. Like everyone, I'm paid in food. When I'm not working, I'm honing my survival skills at school or working on the wall. Now and then I read, usually by sad candlelight.

Two days after the interview, I'm at Elliott's checking inventory when I suddenly feel a tingling in the air. I look up to find Caligula Green staring at me intently.

"Miss Foyle. What a nice surprise."

What's he doing here? I wonder, staring at his unruly hair. There's an auburn streak I don't remember. I look at it closer. *Is that blood?*

"Mr. uh, Green," I stammer and flush head to toe.

He smiles that mysterious little smile again and stares that intense stare. He's wearing a parka, waterproof pants and gloves, and hiking boots. His ski goggles are pulled down around his neck so I can see his hooded eyes. And of course, everything is white, although there are specks of dirt and blood here and there on his sleeves. He looks like he's been skiing but instead of poles he's got a shotgun in a holster across his back and a hatchet strapped to his hip.

In a word, he's breathtaking. I start to pant.

"I need a few things, Miss Foyle."

Like me? My inner sex goddess begins to shimmy.

"Call me Ro," I say. "And how can I do you?" I blush furiously. "I mean, what can I do for you?"

"Roe? Like fish eggs? Bait?" His eyes dance. "How very apt."

What?

He smiles again, then shows me a handful of forms, all signed in triplicate. The guy is authorized to take anything he wants, something I've never seen before. *Does that include me?*

My legs are weak as I help him fill his cart with wire, cables, fully-charged car batteries, saw blades, awls, vises, chains, pulleys, picture hooks, some piano wire and an antique adz.

We pause at one point and he considers an industrial-size level for a few moments. He swings it a few times before carefully putting it in with the rest of his items. He does the same with two hammers and a cheese grater, then checks that a length of climbing rope is sound, and takes all the tape we have.

When I hand him a child's oversized, plastic base-ball bat that he keeps looking at, our fingers briefly touch. Once again, I feel that current, like I'm slowly being elec-trocuted. I stare at the bat, then my eyes stare at him. *Down there.*

Looking up, I notice his lips have curled into that mysterious smile again. *Is he laughing at me?*

"Do you help scavenge the materials as well?" he asks as he pushes his cart down an aisle.

"Scavenging isn't my thing." *I hate going where it's not safe.*

"What is your thing, Aurora?"

"Books." *And you! You! YOU!*

"Stories are a distraction from survival. It's a bad idea to look away from the world around you," he says, suddenly cold and aloof. "How's the article coming?"

"My roommate is writing it. And it's going fine," I tell him. "But she needs a photo of you to go with it. Some-thing heroic."

"I'm around tomorrow," he says. "And I'm always heroic."

"But it's Sunday," I say. "Won't you be busy or something?"

"I hunt every day," he says. "But I'm more than happy to make time for you."

He turns around, and I check out his tight ass again. *Oh my.*

Paul, the fat, greasy bastard who runs the store saunters up. He gives me a long, hard hug.

"How are things going, Ro?" His hand stays draped over my shoulder, lingering like a bad smell. Actually, it is a bad smell. Paul must have run out of soap again.

"I'm with a customer," I say as the men size each other up. I make introductions.

"Not *the* Caligula Green! The zombie killer?" Paul suddenly becomes even more unctuous. "Is there anything I can get you? My sister's in the back. Maybe a quick BJ?"

I look over at Green. He looks intensely angry. I wonder if he's encountered Paul's sister before. Rumor has it, she's a bit of a biter.

"Remove your arm from Miss Foyle's shoulder," he says coldly.

"Huh?" Paul glances at his arm.

Suddenly, Caligula whacks him with the plastic bat. He's fast. His strikes are precise and well-timed, and he's swinging for the fences. The bat comes close to me but I never feel anything but wind. Wham! Bam!

Thank you, ma'am!

Paul is on the ground, bleeding from the nose and mouth, before I can blink. Caligula stands over him. He's not angry, not breathing hard, just protective.

"I'm taking all of this, including the cart. I'll see you tomorrow, Aurora."

Oh my. See you then! I tell him with my eyes. Or maybe my lips. Or in that special girl language that involves twisting your hair around your index finger while you drool. He's a smart guy; he'll figure it out.

I watch as he wheels the cart out of the store. One of his pale helpers, also dressed in white, hurries up to take it off his hands.

Before it looked gross and desiccated. Now it looks exquisite, like art.

"Are you all right?" he asks and we finally shake hands, for real. A current runs through me and I suddenly feel like I'm being electrocuted. It's hard to let go.

"I'm, uh, I'm fine," I stammer, blushing. "I'm Aurora Foyle. I'm studying survival with Penelope Spunk, who was scheduled to interview you." I explain about Pen's food poisoning and he nods, his eyes hooded.

"Sit." He gestures to a white leather couch.

I look around at the furniture, the carpet, the coffee table. Everything is white, which must be hard to pull off when your job keeps you covered in blood and gore. I stare at him as I take a seat on the couch, which smells delicious. Like candy. Then I realize, it's not the couch, it's him. He not only gorgeous, he's clean. Completely clean. *Probably even down there.*

I'd trade this guy whatever he wanted for a rotten burger, I think, then immediately blush deep red. From the other room, I hear that groaning sound again. Must be some kind of training seminar next door.

When I look up, I see that his eyes are on me. He's watching me intently, but not in the leering way men watch Penelope. I lean forward to pull my roommate's carefully prepared questions and a notebook and pen out of my satchel. He doesn't even seem to notice my boobs spilling out of my impossibly tight top.

"This interview will, uh, appear in the Survival School newsletter," I mumble. My heartbeat speeds up.

"Yes, I know. I'm handing out the degrees at your graduation," he says. "I also designed the curriculum. And convinced the council to build the school five years ago."

He's completely deadpan. *Does that come in handy in his line of work?*

I blush again and stare down at Pen's questions, trying to ignore the sounds from the next room.

Focus, Ro, focus!

"You've killed more zombies than anyone. Why are you still alive?"

I look up at him, my pen poised.

"I know the dead, Miss Foyle," he says matter-of-factly. "How they move, where they'll be, which will attack first if they're in a group. I know when to use an axe, when to use a bullet, and when to simply get out of the way."

The world seems to stop as he leans forward.

"I also know what the dead are drawn to." His eyes are looking me up and down and I blush again. *Maybe I do have a shot.*

I swallow. "Are you just lucky?"

Would you like to get lucky?

He smiles a tight, mysterious smile. "I don't believe in luck, Miss Foyle. I work hard. I make quick decisions. I employ albinos. I also stay in shape, eat right, and use good tools." His eyes are pools of green, like ponds covered in algae.

My inner sex goddess quickly gets a Brazilian wax and puts on a bikini. She's ready to dive right in.

He looks out the window, inviting me to study his profile. "I also control my fear so that I never hesitate."

"Do you enjoy control?"

"No. But in my line of work it pays to be ready. And to understand all my options."

"Do you feel immensely powerful?" *Or do you just look it?*

"I employ forty people. I do my best to keep another 4,000 safe so that they can rebuild what's left of their lives."

He smiles and his teeth gleam. "I feel good about myself."

Our last tube of toothpaste ran out days ago, and we won't be allocated another for three weeks. I briefly consider using his bathroom in order to stock up on supplies. *I'd love to get my hands on that hair gel!*

I quickly dismiss the idea and look down at my questions. "Do you answer to the ruling counsel?"

He leans toward me. "I don't answer to anyone, Miss Foyle. I put the undead down and I keep the supplies coming and in return, the counsel gives me whatever I want. Eventually, everyone gives me what I want."

I gasp, then blush, then bite my lip, realizing that I'm blushing. *Breathe, Ro, breathe!* I stare down at Pen's questions, rattled.

"Um, do you do anything besides work?" *Because there are a few things I'd like to do right now.*

"I have varied interests: music, pole vaulting, fifteenth century instruments of torture. Don't we all? But mainly I work. I build things. I help people figure out how to grow food. I reinforce the wall. I make sure we're as safe as we can be. I want to survive."

"Me, too," I whisper and flush again. He leans forward, suddenly more interested.

"What are you willing to do to help others survive?" he asks, his eyes growing impossibly intense.

"Well, I'm ... uh ... I'm about to graduate," I stammer. "I guess I'll use my skills to the best of my ability, like everyone's expected to."

"Of course you will," he says. "Just as I use my skills to the best of *my* ability."

"To help others survive?"

"Yes," he says after a brief pause.

I start to wonder if the rumors are true. Maybe Green really is working on trying to find a cure for this whole zombie thing.

"You, uh, you have a lot of nice stuff," I say, looking around. "The nicest."

"I deserve all of it," he says, leaning back. "I've worked hard for it. Killed for it. And nearly been killed a thousand times. Every day is Black Friday beyond the wall."

He smiles that bemused smile again and my inner smart ass blows a raspberry. The guy is full of himself. *I'd love to be full of him, too, though.*

"Are you important, Mr. Green?" I stare at the question again. "Oops, I mean, are you impotent?"

He inhales sharply and his eyes darken, then blaze, then cool, then cut me to the quick with indifference. *Damn you, Penelope Spunk!*

"No," he answers coldly.

"I'm sorry," I say, nodding at the paper. "That was one of Penelope's questions."

I wonder about his answer, though. He hasn't even glanced at my boobs, despite the fact my left nipple has wiggled its way out of the latex jacket. I swear it's like they have a life of their own.

Just then a white head pokes through the doorway and tells Green he has another appointment. I get up, convinced that I'm about to be given the boot, but instead he cancels his meeting.

The albino Barbie stares at me and raises what would be her eyebrows, if she had eyebrows. *Holy cow. He wants me to stay?*

"I'd like to know about you, Miss Foyle," he says, gesturing me to sit again. "It's only fair."

"There's not much to tell." I flush and immediately, there's that weird moaning sound from the room next door. He leans forward, almost eagerly.

"What are you going to do after you graduate?" He stares at me intently as he rakes his hand through his stunningly unruly hair.

I'm suddenly very warm. *Down there.* "I'll probably get a job in agriculture," I tell him. "Most of my friends are going to be farmers." Except Penelope who wants to become a black market kingpin. Or a cruise director.

"Your gifts would be wasted with all those hoes." His lips curl into a smile. "You should come work with me. Outside the wall. It's quite ... stimulating."

"I'm not sure I'd be able to do that," I mumble. *I'm uncoordinated and unkempt and my body produces pigment.* "I'm sure I'd get bitten."

"Oh, I'd keep you safe."

His voice is dead serious and I believe him. My insides melt a little and my inner child hugs herself and smiles beatifically. *Safe!* "Thanks. I'll, uh, I'll think about it."

"You'd have everything you could ever want."

"You could have anything you want right now," I say, lowering my eyes and looking up at him submissively through my thick auburn lashes. Pen and I have spent hours perfecting that move. But he doesn't even notice. It's like I'm offering him a hammer.

"I'm not interested in sex, Miss Foyle," he says. "I'm only interested in the undead. And I want you to come work with me when I hunt them. You're a talented young woman. I'd love to take advantage of your talents."

Holy fuck. At least he wants me for something. But I need to think about this. I stand up.

"Thank you for the interview, Mr. Green. And the job offer."

"The pleasure has been all mine, Miss Foyle."

CHAPTER TWO

My heart is hammering as I leave the elevator of his building and rush outside. I actually welcome the scent of decay, the putrid breath of the city. It helps me recover from the last few, surreal minutes.

No one has ever looked at me the way Caligula Green looked at me. There was no lust in his eyes, but there was raw unadulterated *something*.

What's his deal?

I made it clear I wanted to be his plaything, but all he seems to want is somebody to reload his shotgun. *And not in a good way.*

And what's with all that stuff about keeping me safe. Wouldn't it be safer to take a farming job than to press my luck as a junior zombie hunter?

Forget it, Ro. Put that all behind you. But the interview continues to eat at me as I head home. Thankfully, it's the only thing.

Penelope and I live in a basement apartment in Pioneer Square, about a half mile from the school. It's dark and dank and still pretty gross. It was once used as storage for the garage next door so there aren't many windows, and the only door is heavily reinforced. I don't mind that we don't have a view. If you can see out, the zombies can get in. Plus, who wants to look at a wasteland?

Pen is sharpening her knives -- literally -- when I walk through the door. The kitchen table is covered with ropes, each one sporting a different knot. In the corner, I see a few tires she's "attacked," covered with cuts and stab marks. She's been studying for finals and looks like she's feeling better.

"You're back! How did it go? What was he like?"

I toss my notebook to her. "Intimidating. Sexy as hell. Dressed all in white. Cold and entirely uninterested in breasts or other body parts." *Any living part, that is. I think back on the severed hand.*

"Who wouldn't want those breasts? Or those lips?" Pen asks, bewildered.

I shrug. "I know, right?"

"Jeez, Ro, maybe he really is impotent. I mean, that's always been the rumor because he's so driven and only seems to think about killing zombies. Most men don't have that kind of focus."

"I know," I say, trying to escape to my room where I can masturbate in peace. But it's impossible to put off Penelope and her persistent questions. I end up telling her about the interview.

"I can't believe you didn't take him up on his job offer," she says when I finish. "You'd have been famous *and* well-fed."

"And dead. Or worse."

I look over at our wind-up alarm clock and realize I'm late for work at the hardware store. My inner time-keeper looks at her wrist then taps her foot impatiently.

"Holy cow! I have to run, Pen. Feel better!"

* * *

Elliott Bay Salvage isn't really a hardware store but that's the closest word that describes the place. Back in the day, it used to be a bookstore, full of creaky wooden stairs, lofts and isolated cubbyholes. Now every corner is full of recycled or reclaimed crap: faucet heads, hammers, dolls, espresso machine parts. There are lots of tools, too, not to mention tools looking for tools and salvaged building materials. We also stock bicycle parts, kitchen supplies, and bits and pieces scrounged from cars: seat belts, suitcases, and personal items pulled from trunks and glove compartments.

Lots of people thought they could outrun the virus. They were wrong.

The store, and others like it, has teams working all over the city and even outside the wall scavenging whatever useful items they can find. Until we start manufacturing things again, we have to make use of every board and nail. Thanks to the zombies, Seattle finally became the recycling paradise it always wanted to be.

We're always busy, mostly with turning away folks who want what we have in stock but don't have the authorization to take it. The council controls all resources. Things were much easier when we used money but then people realized money was pretty worthless. Now you need a ration card or a form signed in triplicate to "buy" anything, even the sad little crayon candles my mother squishes together.

Unless you want to barter, like Pen.

I work at Elliott's a few hours every day. Like everyone, I'm paid in food. When I'm not working, I'm honing my survival skills at school or working on the wall. Now and then I read, usually by sad candlelight.

Two days after the interview, I'm at Elliott's checking inventory when I suddenly feel a tingling in the air. I look up to find Caligula Green staring at me intently.

"Miss Foyle. What a nice surprise."

What's he doing here? I wonder, staring at his unruly hair. There's an auburn streak I don't remember. I look at it closer. *Is that blood?*

"Mr. uh, Green," I stammer and flush head to toe.

He smiles that mysterious little smile again and stares that intense stare. He's wearing a parka, water-proof pants and gloves, and hiking boots. His ski goggles are pulled down around his neck so I can see his hooded eyes. And of course, everything is white, although there are specks of dirt and blood here and there on his sleeves. He looks like he's been skiing but instead of poles he's got a shotgun in a holster across his back and a hatchet strapped to his hip.

In a word, he's breathtaking. I start to pant.

"I need a few things, Miss Foyle."

Like me? My inner sex goddess begins to shimmy.

"Call me Ro," I say. "And how can I do you?" I blush furiously. "I mean, what can I do for you?"

"Roe? Like fish eggs? Bait?" His eyes dance. "How very apt."

What?

He smiles again, then shows me a handful of forms, all signed in triplicate. The guy is authorized to take any-thing he wants, something I've never seen before. *Does that include me?*

My legs are weak as I help him fill his cart with wire, cables, fully-charged car batteries, saw blades, awls, vises, chains, pulleys, picture hooks, some piano wire and an antique adz.

We pause at one point and he considers an industrial-size level for a few moments. He swings it a few times before carefully putting it in with the rest of his items. He does the same with two hammers and a cheese grater, then checks that a length of climbing rope is sound, and takes all the tape we have.

When I hand him a child's oversized, plastic baseball bat that he keeps looking at, our fingers briefly touch. Once again, I feel that current, like I'm slowly being electrocuted. I stare at the bat, then my eyes stare at him. *Down there.*

Looking up, I notice his lips have curled into that mysterious smile again. *Is he laughing at me?*

"Do you help scavenge the materials as well?" he asks as he pushes his cart down an aisle.

"Scavenging isn't my thing." *I hate going where it's not safe.*

"What is your thing, Aurora?"

"Books." *And you! You! YOU!*

"Stories are a distraction from survival. It's a bad idea to look away from the world around you," he says, suddenly cold and aloof. "How's the article coming?"

"My roommate is writing it. And it's going fine," I tell him. "But she needs a photo of you to go with it. Something heroic."

"I'm around tomorrow," he says. "And I'm always heroic."

"But it's Sunday," I say. "Won't you be busy or something?"

"I hunt every day," he says. "But I'm more than happy to make time for you."

He turns around, and I check out his tight ass again. *Oh my.*

Paul, the fat, greasy bastard who runs the store saunters up. He gives me a long, hard hug.

"How are things going, Ro?" His hand stays draped over my shoulder, lingering like a bad smell. Actually, it is a bad smell. Paul must have run out of soap again.

"I'm with a customer," I say as the men size each other up. I make introductions.

"Not *the* Caligula Green! The zombie killer?" Paul suddenly becomes even more unctuous. "Is there anything I can get you? My sister's in the back. Maybe a quick BJ?"

I look over at Green. He looks intensely angry. I wonder if he's encountered Paul's sister before. Rumor has it, she's a bit of a biter.

"Remove your arm from Miss Foyle's shoulder," he says coldly.

"Huh?" Paul glances at his arm.

Suddenly, Caligula whacks him with the plastic bat. He's fast. His strikes are precise and well-timed, and he's swinging for the fences. The bat comes close to me but I never feel anything but wind. Wham! Bam!

Thank you, ma'am!

Paul is on the ground, bleeding from the nose and mouth, before I can blink. Caligula stands over him. He's not angry, not breathing hard, just protective.

"I'm taking all of this, including the cart. I'll see you tomorrow, Aurora."

Oh my. See you then! I tell him with my eyes. Or maybe my lips. Or in that special girl language that involves twisting your hair around your index finger while you drool. He's a smart guy; he'll figure it out.

I watch as he wheels the cart out of the store. One of his pale helpers, also dressed in white, hurries up to take it off his hands.

I turn and help Paul up. Pinching his nose to stop the blood, he disappears into the back room without a word.

* * *

At home, I'm working on an essay on Matheson's *I Am Legend* when there's a knock on the door. It's our friend Hoser. He's the only Canadian behind the wall, and maybe the only one left in the world. He's got a six-pack of Molson and a wicked grin.

"Who did you have to sleep with to get that?"

"Don't ask." He looks a little self-conscious. Probably the old lady with the gun collection and scabies. Poor Hoser.

"I have news," he says. "I got the okay from the counsel to open an art gallery. I just have to make sure I put in the same amount of hours on the wall."

"Congratulations!" I scream and give him a full body hug. He hugs me back. We're just friends, but I know that he wants more, and that's why he brought the beer. But I'm just not attracted to him like that. He's like a brother to me.

Which is why we only dry hump -- although we always manage to come simultaneously. Afterward, I ask if he can take a photo of Green the next day. Naturally, he says yes.

We start dry humping again and I come immensely and immediately, thinking of Green's tight ass as he rolled his shopping cart away.

Oh my.

CHAPTER THREE

"He came there because he totally wants you, Ro," Pen tells me the next morning after I tell her about Green's visit to Elliott's.

"He just needed a few things," I tell her.

"And you're one of them," she tells me.

I shrug, tellingly.

"He did beat up Paul, that guy who's always trying to get me into bed. But I think he was just trying to be nice."

But deep down, I know Caligula Green doesn't do nice.

Pen and I practice widening our eyes, biting our lips and twisting our hair around our fingers for a while and then I head to the store for a few hours. I'm sorting screws when Paul comes up behind me, making noise so that I know he's there. When I turn he has his arms up, like he's surrendering. His face is bruised purple and blue and there's still fresh blood under the bandage above his eyebrow.

"So, you know Caligula Green."

"Yep."

"Please apologize to him for me. Make it sincere."

"Sure."

"And let me know if I can buy you a drink to make it up to you," he leers.

I pick a length of PVC pipe and level him with a stare. I don't see him again for the rest of the morning.

* * *

After work, I head home to get ready for the photo shoot. Hoser's already there, sweaty from rushing over. He's got his best camera, a digital SLR with a pristine lens.

"I recharged the batteries last night, before the power cut out," he says. "Smart, eh? They should hold up for a while. As long as we work outside so I don't need the flash."

Pen turns to me. "Where are we meeting Green?"

"I'm not sure. He agreed on today. But we didn't really fix a time or place." My mind goes back to the sight of his muscles bulging under his white parka as he took the baseball bat to Paul. Logistics aren't exactly my strong suit, especially when I'm distracted.

"Ro, you're the one in a relationship with him."

I'm about to protest when we're interrupted by a knock on the door. I open it.

Caligula Green is standing there in all of his white-clad glory. He's got his usual weapons: axe, shotgun, piercing eyes. And, in his left hand, he's holding the pink baseball bat.

"Miss Foyle. How nice to see you again."

Is he stalking me? How does he know where I live?

"It's Aurora," I say. "And what are you doing here? Especially right now? We were just getting ready for the photo shoot."

"I told you I would be around today," he says, raising a long-fingered hand into the air like a magician. He snaps his fingers. "Voila! Here I am."

I'm completely flustered. *And I'm also completely turned on.* But this beautiful man is only interested in saving mankind. Talk about frustrating.

I blush furiously, wondering if he can read my thoughts.

That seems to get his attention. His eyes blaze and he looks me up and down. There's something going on behind his eyes. *And maybe down there, in the secret sex place deep in his pants!*

"She only blushes like that when she likes someone," Pen says behind me. "I've never seen her so affected."

"Pen, I blush all the time!" I stammer, then quickly introduce the two of them.

"The tenacious Miss Spunk. How are you feeling today?"

"Fine, thanks." She shakes his hand and bats her eyes at him. Pen's beauty and commanding presence usually attract men like maggots to a damp corpse. Green hardly notices her.

"And this is Hoser Vancouver, our photographer."

"Mr. Green," Hoser nods.

Green's expression changes. He studies Hoser's brow, then reaches up with a finger and wipes off some sweat. He holds his finger under his nose and takes a deep sniff.

"You've been bitten," he says. "But you have some time. Maybe five days."

"You're full of it," Hoser says, taking a step back. "I think I'd remember if I was bitten, eh?"

"Yes. I almost believe you," Green says calmly. "Which is why I'm not killing you now."

He pats the hatchet on his belt. "See you in a few days."

Holy crap. The guy has the sickest sense of humor in the world!

* * *

We decide to head over to Occidental Park for the photo shoot, since it's close and looks a lot like the wasteland on the other side of the wall. The only difference: no zombies. Well, at least none that are still walking. *I hope.* You still have to be careful, of course. Even with the nightly patrols, strays can appear anywhere.

We set up in front of a storefront by an overturned Beetle. Its roof is crushed, its bulk smashed into a brick wall. Two desiccated skeletons slump in the seats inside the car. Another body, headless, lies by the glassless front door. Dead zombie.

Redundant! my inner schoolmarm chides, pointing to a blackboard covered with sentence diagrams.

I ignore her and glance inside the store. There are a few remains scattered here and there. Some have a bit of meat, most have none. The wall are spattered with old blood. Looks like there was a feeding frenzy here at some point.

"Where would you like me?" Green asks.

How about between my legs for starters?

"Just in front of the window to start," Pen barks, going into art director mode. "Lose the silly bat. And hold that hatchet like you mean it, mister."

Hoser starts to snap away while Green poses with his arm up, axe poised, and his arm down, axe at his side. He never smiles. He looks alert, like he's ready for anything to come at him. But the intense pictures -- the keepers -- are the ones where he looks directly at Hoser. His eyes blaze with an intensity that makes me feel all squishy and achy inside, like I have a bladder infection coming on.

I gasp as the sun moves from behind a cloud and strikes his clothes. Green looks angelic. He positively glows. *Like the angel of death.*

"I think we have enough," Hoser announces after about twenty minutes. "I just wish you were holding a shinier, bigger axe."

"Trafalgar!" Green shouts.

Seconds later, the muscular albino with the boots from Green's building rounds the corner. In his hand is a large, polished, two-headed axe.

"Is this what you'd have me use?" There's menace in Green's voice. "Now?" His voice drops, and he stares intently at Hoser. "And later, when your time comes?"

Hoser is sweating again. He swallows hard, then puts his camera to his eye and snaps a few more pictures.

"Yeah, that's perfect," he says. He shoots a few more then nods at Penelope.

"Thank you again, Mr. Green," she says, coming forward to shake his hand. Hoser hangs back, silent.

"My pleasure," he says, then turns to me. "Will you walk with me, Miss Foyle?"

Green leaves Pen and Hoser standing in the street, and we head northeast. The albino follows us.

"See you tomorrow morning, Ro!" Pen calls over her shoulder. I turn and watch them head back toward our apartment. Hoser looks a little depressed.

"Would you like some coffee?" Green asks.

Coffee? Holy cow. And he probably has the real thing!

"That, that would be delightful," I stammer. The city ran out of fresh coffee before gasoline, penicillin and hair gel. We should have had enough to last 100 years but once people realized there was a finite amount, they started drinking it like crazy -- which I guess explains how the wall was built so quickly.

I hadn't had real coffee in three years, although Pen and I had been experimenting with a mix of black market used grounds and dry leaves that wasn't too bad.

We step into a wreck of a cafe two blocks away. It's in the ground floor of an office building. The albino uncovers an overturned table and two intact chairs, then grabs everything and follows us. Green has a powerful flashlight that he's pulled from some interior pocket.

Is that a flashlight in your pocket or are you just glad to see me? my inner sex goddess asks. *Shut it, you twit!* my subconscious counters. *We could get killed here. This is a prime roamer hiding spot!*

I follow Green through what used to be the lobby, trying to ignore the voices in my head. There are footprints in the dust leading through a waiting area. Someone or something tore the leather furniture apart, probably looking for a meal. There's foam everywhere. Green leads me to a bank of elevators. Not surprisingly, none of them work.

He forces the first set of doors apart. He doesn't strain, but I can't help think of his muscles working under his raincoat. An empty shaft yawns before us.

Shaft. What a lovely word.

I look to the side and the albino is unreadable, quietly holding the cafe table and chairs.

The doors to the next elevator are already open. It contains the remains of two corpses locked in what may have been a final embrace. They still have their heads so they must have died naturally. *Suicide?*

Caligula forces the third elevator's doors open, and we see a man staring out at us. He's filthy, surrounded by garbage. As the doors open, he scuttles to the back of the car, trying to hide beneath a stack of mannequins. I look closer. They're life-size sex dolls.

He breaks into a chant, "Don't eat me! Don't judge me! Don't eat me! Don't judge me!" Green takes the time to force these doors closed again.

"What is it about elevators?" I ask.

"They're safe, Miss Foyle. Three impenetrable walls make a very good home. Ah, here we are."

The fourth elevator is empty. The albino sets down the table and chairs and dusts them off with a handkerchief. On top of the table, he places a lit candle that smells like vanilla, two clean cups, and a steaming thermos of coffee that smells *way* better than our used Yuban. I'm not sure where the albino was hiding it. *I probably don't want to know.*

Green takes my hand and leads me to the cleaner of the two seats. I feel that unmistakable current running through me again, all the way down to my achy lady parts, and for a moment I wonder if the elevator might have power after all. Then I realize it's Green. *The man is electric!*

There's a giggle from the elevator next door. Sounds like a threesome is getting started.

Hmmm. Now there's an idea.

We ignore the sounds and sit while the albino forces our elevator's door closed. Suddenly we're alone in our own world: coffee and vanilla and candlelight. Even in the reflection of the dirty metal walls, I can see that my hair looks like crap. *Yet again.* And of course Green looks spectacular: all piercing eyes and chiseled cheekbones. He doesn't seem to notice my hair. And he hasn't let go of my hand since we entered the elevator, which means I can't do anything to fix it.

He suddenly pulls his hand away *as if reading my mind!* And pours us both coffee.

"Cup of real coffee for your thoughts?"

I smile and take a sip. It must be stale, like everything that's been sitting around since the zombies took over, but to me, it tastes heavenly. I resist the urge to ask if it's fair trade, organic, and shade grown.

"Thank you again for doing the shoot," I stammer. "The article wouldn't be the same without a photo of you. And everyone is so, uh, I mean we students have heard so much about--"

"So, is the photographer your boyfriend?" Green interrupts, staring at me intensely. The steam from his coffee makes his eyes flicker.

"Hoser? No, he's just a friend," I tell him, flushing. "Well, he's more like family, really. Like a brother. Or a cousin. But not a kissing cousin. I've never kissed him."

Not on the mouth, anyway.

"And your friend at the store?"

"Paul?" I say with a shudder. "He's just my boss." I rerun the memory of Green knocking the shit out of Paul with the toy baseball bat and flush.

"You seem violent around men," I say, gathering up my courage. "Or at least around the men in my life."

"It's in my nature to take care of problems," Green says.

"Do you consider the men in my life problems?"

Green simply smiles and sips his coffee.

I suddenly flush with anger. "I don't understand why you feel it's necessary to go around intimidating everyone," I fume. "That thing you said to Hoser. He thought you were serious. You scared him!"

"I was serious," he says quietly. "Aurora, I'm dangerous. Your friends *should* be intimidated." He sips his coffee. "As should you."

I continue to flush deep red and look at my hands. Off in the distance, I hear something. A low moan?

Green seems to tense for a moment, as if he hears it, too, then looks at me and slowly relaxes.

"You fascinate me, Miss Foyle. You're very ... alluring."

Me? Alluring? I'm used to having men slobber all over Penelope. My inner sex goddess starts doing a slow bump and grind, a wide smile on her face.

"I'm glad you find me interesting," I say, leaning closer. My hand reaches out to touch his knee. "I find you, uh, I mean, I'd like to have, you know you can do anything you want to me."

"I want to take you outside the walls."

Except that! My hand jerks away from his knee, and I sit upright, silently shaking my head.

"I'm used to getting my way, Aurora."

"You want to take me into the heart of Zombieville when you haven't even asked me to call you by your first name?" I squeak. "I don't think so, mister. I mean, Mr. Green."

"Please, do call me Caligula. And tell me a little about yourself. About your parents."

I look at him in exasperation. One minute, he's a cold-blooded killer, ready to hack apart my friend. The next he's an over-solicitous suitor.

How adorable can one man get?

"Well, my mom's still alive although she's not ... well," I say. "She lives north of downtown, although she thinks she's still living back home in Georgia. She used to be a kindergarten teacher there. Now, she makes candles out of leftover crayons and anything else she can scavenge. She may have even made this one." I gesture at the table and the two of us consider the vanilla candle in front of us.

"Everyone else is dead," I tell him after a moment. "What about you? Where's your family?"

"Undead," he snaps. It's a conversation stopper.

I sip my coffee and watch him pick at a piece of dried skin on his lower lip. *Oh my.*

"Perhaps you can meet them sometime," he says, after a moment.

Huh?

He takes a final sip of coffee and as if on cue, the albino opens the doors. We get up as his manservant gathers the coffee things. Then we walk out of the building into the light of the street.

"Do you want a girlfriend?" I blurt out. "Or maybe just a fuck buddy or something?" *Crap. Did I just say that?* My subconscious, my inner sex goddess and my inner child all gape at each other in amazement.

"I don't do the emotional thing," he says, looking at me with bemusement. "Or the physical thing, either. But I do want to take care of you. You need protecting, Aurora."

We pause between two cars. They almost look drivable. Green grabs my arm and turns me around so he can look at my butt.

"Do you always wear leather boots and jeans?" he says, staring at my ass. *I hope.*

I blush. "Well, not always." I look up at him through my lashes, demurely. *Sometimes I wear tiny bits of rubber that I find in the garage back home. Other times, Pen and I run around in welding masks and nothing else.*

"You should," he continues. "Boots are good for kicking and they protect your ankles. And denim is hard to bite through. *Always* wear clothing that is hard to bite through."

I turn, embarrassed, and step toward the street. *I have to get away from him. He's just too pragmatic. Not to mention phlegmatic. Plus I thoroughly embarrassed myself with that whole, "Do you want a girlfriend?" thing.* I roll my eyes and kick at a rock.

Suddenly, something grabs my ankle, and I fall to my knees. It's a legless crawler with one good hand. The guts trailing behind it are hard and dry. It was hiding under one of the cars. And now it's doing its best to gnaw through my boots.

"Aurora!" Green cries, seeing it. He lunges at me, pulls me onto my feet by one arm, and I fall back toward him. He's got his hatchet out. It swings past me and smashes the thing's skull in. End of attack.

He takes me in his arms. I take a second to inhale his cleanliness. He's a fresh load of laundry in a world full of rotting rags.

It's intoxicating. *Oh my.*

"I'm okay," I whisper. He still has his arm around me, but his eyes are on the street.

He nods, then thoroughly inspects my foot and leg.

"No really. It didn't bite me," I tell him.

He finishes, then holds my head in both hands, searching my face.

"When someone is going to turn, you can see it first in the eyes," he says. "The hunger."

He's looking into my eyes. He has a beautiful mouth, even with his chapped lips. His teeth are as white as his servants' hair and skin. *I wouldn't mind if he bit me on the foot. Or anywhere else.*

CHAPTER FOUR

Caligula is holding me. *Bite me, damn it!* I implore him. I blush, warmed by the current that runs between us. And then I see what I think is hunger in his eyes. Not zombie hunger, or hunger hunger, but something else. Something more primal. He's breathing hard. He looks like he's about to lose it. I will myself closer to his mouth. *Oh, to kiss those chapped lips!*

He closes his eyes and breathes deeply, regaining control. When he opens his eyes again, they're cold.

"Miss Foyle, you should be more careful," he chides, softly. "The world is too dangerous for the likes of you."

He pulls me closer and for a moment, I think I feel something move. *Down there.*

"You need to stay close to me," he says. "I'm the only one who can protect you." Then he lets me go and gently pushes me away.

"I want more than just protection," I say, feeling foolish, yet exhilarated. And also a little hungry. Not to mention pretty darn concerned about my unruly hair. *It's not easy being a girl in a post-apocalyptic world.*

"I'm sorry," I tell him, flustered. "I've never been attacked like that before."

"If you listen to me, you never will again," he says, his voice husky. "I want you, Aurora."

Hot damn! I gasp and look up at him, hopefully. Then cast a surreptitious eye at the car next to us. The back seat isn't too filthy. It could do in a pinch.

"I want you to work for me."

My shoulders droop. *Oh well. At least he wants me for something.*

"Thanks for saving me," I mutter. "I guess you can't hire me if I'm dead."

He stares down at me, his face softening.

"Saving people is what I do, Aurora," he says. "And it's what I'm going to continue to do with you. Because even if you're not working for me -- working *with* me -- they're going to come for you."

What? "I don't understand. Why would--?"

"You're welcome for the photo shoot, by the way," he interrupts. "Now let's get you home. I need to get a cleanup crew here to take care of this infectious mess."

He gestures at the crawler, and I nod wordlessly.

He walks me back to my apartment as if he's on security detail. He's all control, scanning the debris, weapon in hand as if he's expecting another attack at any moment. I disappear into my place without a word, then fall to my knees by the couch.

Why am I bawling? I hug myself closer, listening to Penelope and Hoser going at it in the other room. She's probably thanking him for the photo shoot. At least their moaning hides my sobs.

I've never come so close to being bit before. Plus, I've never been rejected. By anybody. Guys seem to love me, even when I don't have Pen's help getting dressed. I'm fit, I'm healthy, I've got clear skin and a nice rack. My hair's a complete disaster but deep down I know that men are irresistibly drawn to complete disasters. Every man but Caligula Green.

Why doesn't he want me? I wail again into a throw pillow. *Why won't he even kiss me! All he thinks about is his stupid job.*

My sobs begin to subside as my internal career counselor takes over. Green is offering me a tremendous opportunity. The man has access to the best the city has to offer. *His assistants gave me ice!*

Trust him and you'll end up on ice! my inner lifeguard warns.

I let my inner pals hash it out while I pull dry pieces of dandruff from my sweater. I put them on the floor in front of me, trying to make a capital "G."

That's where Pen finds me a few minutes later. Hoser must be taking a nap.

"What's wrong?" she asks, seeing my tears. "Was the sex that awful?"

"We didn't do anything," I tell her, then begin to sob again. "A zombie nearly bit me. Green saved me."

"Jeez, are you okay?"

She runs her fingers through my hair and looks at me. I nod.

"How was the coffee?" she asks. "I *know* you had real coffee. You reek of it."

I tell her about the coffee, the attentive albino, the doll fucker, our sweet little elevator café. She's intrigued.

"But he's not interested in me, Pen," I say at last. "I don't think he's interested in anyone. Anyone living that is."

Pen just stares at me.

"Who cares," she says at last. "Take the fucking job. Maybe he'll pay you in coffee."

"But I don't want to go outside the wall, Pen," I whisper. "It's not safe."

"Safe?" she scoffs. "You were attacked three blocks from where you live. There is no safe."

I sigh and begin to play with my hair. It's my go-to place. Pen pulls Hoser's camera off the table and shows me some of the pictures from the shoot. Green is magnificent. He looks like he could take on a zombie horde of any size. He also looks like the kind of man who can have anyone he wants. I suddenly understand why he doesn't want me.

"Maybe he'd be a good boss," I say after a while.

Pen nods and pats me on the head, and I go off to take a nap. *I don't do the emotional thing. Or the physical one, either,* he said. Maybe he lied about the impotence thing. Lots of people got sucked in by quacks promising to keep them safe from the zombie virus. Erections weren't the only things people lost.

I shudder, trying to imagine what it would be like to have a penis that refused to respond to stimulation. But I felt something large *down there* when he had his arm around me. It may have been a flashlight. Or maybe Green has other problems. *PTSD?*

I dream of running through the woods, barefoot, that night. The hands of the dead emerge from beneath the leafy forest floor, grabbing at me. I see a white-clad figure in the distance. As he raises his axe, I'm not sure if he's going to kill me or save me.

Waking, I realize I don't care. I'm coming like a motherfucker.

* * *

Five days later, it's Friday and finals are over. *Woo hoo!*

I slog home, tired from a day of hacking, running, dodging and knot-tying to find a package in front of my door.

Inside, I find two boxes. One contains a handgun with a full clip. It's been bedazzled and sparkles like his eyes. I don't know a thing about guns, but it feels like it was made for my hand. There's also a brand new media player, pristine in its original box, with fully charged batteries. It's white, of course, with matching headphones, and loaded with classic zombie movies. I feel bad about leaving fingerprints on it.

On a plain white card there's a quote from *Dawn of the Dead*: "We must think logically. We must deal with this crisis logically, with calm and unemotional response. We have to remain rational. We have to remain logical."

I recognize the quote because I just wrote an essay about the best way to stay safe in an unsecured shopping mall. My answer involved a lot of hiding in the ceiling.

Pen looks over my shoulder.

"Holy shit. That stuff is worth a fortune! Green?"

I nod.

"If you don't take that job right fucking now I'm going to kill you myself. He's into you even if he's not *in* you!"

I put the gun in one pocket, the media player in the other, and I head out with Pen to meet up with Hoser to celebrate the end of school in time-honored fashion: by getting wasted.

Pen is all heels and tight jeans; even her unkempt greasy hair looks awesome. I'm a little chilly in my T-shirt and tennis shoes but I'll be damned if I'm going to let a control freak dictate what I wear.

"To the end of exams and the beginning of life!" We toast each other over a few shots of rotgut. The local pub ferments whatever they can throw into the vat -- grass, kelp, corn, Astroturf -- and it tastes like death. But good booze is impossible to find. That ran out right after the coffee.

"So what now, Ro?" Hoser asks. He hasn't had a drink all night, but his eyes are red and he's pale. He's sweating too much and keeps pulling down the sleeves of his shirt, like he's got the chills. Which is weird because no one gets sick these days. The zombie virus killed most of the other microbes and bacteria. That's why dead bodies take so long to rot. On the upside, though, STDs are pretty much nonexistent. Unfortunately, so are babies -- it's harder than hell to get pregnant. So much for repopulating the world.

"I guess I'm going to pull weeds." I smile. I find it sweet that Hoser is so nervous around me.

He puts his arm around me. "You deserve so much more than that. I'd like to give you more."

It's too much for me. I shrug him off and stumble to the bathroom. When I push open the door to the women's room, I find Green standing in front of me in another pure white ensemble.

"Aurora."

"What the hell?" I slur. "What are you doing in the women's bathroom? And why did you send me all that stuff?"

He stares at me for a moment, then leans forward. I think he's going to kiss me but he simply smells my breath.

"You've had too much to drink," he says sourly. Behind him, on the wall, an ad on the front of an old condom dispenser is extolling the virtues of dispensable options for her pleasure. *What about my pleasure?*

I push past him and head into a stall, slamming the door.

"You need to stay in control of yourself," he says through the door as I pee. "It's the only way to survive."

I finish up and push past him, ignoring the filthy sink. I don't need a lecture. *I need someone to do me. To help me forget the horrible world we live in.* I stomp back to our table, grab Hoser, and head outside.

It's cooler there. Unfortunately, the abandoned cars seem to be spinning for some reason.

"I think I've had a bit too much to drink," I say weakly, trying to focus on my friend. He looks awful; his face is positively green. "Hoser, what's wrong?"

"Ro, please." He's got me in his arms. *This is more like it.* "I'm losing control."

I reach for his zipper. "I am, too, baby. Let's lose it together."

"I've always loved you, Ro. But it's too late now!" He tries to push me away, but I won't budge. No way am I going to put up with another rejection today.

"Come on, Hoser," I say, taking his hand and placing it on my breast. He looks at me, tortured.

"You've got to get out of here! Away from me, eh?" Suddenly, he cries out and doubles over, clutching his stomach. Then he starts to convulse and drops to his knees. After a second, he slumps onto the ground. He's still. I don't move, either.

"Hoser?"

A few moments go by and I lean down and nudge his shoulder. He makes a sound, and I breathe a sigh of relief.

"Hoser, you scared the shit out of me," I say.

Suddenly, he sits up, then lurches to his feet. He turns and lunges at me passionately. He grabs my hair and pulls my face toward him. His mouth is open. He's moaning already. *He's totally into me!*

I look down just as our mouths are about to meet and see that his sleeve is no longer pulled down around his wrist. It's pushed up and there's a big chunk of flesh missing from his left forearm. A bite-sized chunk.

Green was right! He's been bit!

I look into his face and it's like looking at a stuffed Hoser doll. *His eyes aren't just glassy. They're dead.* His teeth are coming for me.

"Hoser, no!" I try to push him away but the thing that was my friend clutches me tighter, trying to dig its incisors into the side of my face. His lips leave cool kisses on my cheek. If his teeth break my skin, it's game over.

"I think she said no," a voice in the dark says. Then there's the thunk of a hatchet and I feel Hoser's body slump. Gray matter and blood spatter my face and clothes, and I spit out a small, hairy chunk of my former friend's skull.

I get out from under the corpse and stumble back, away from the pile of flesh and fresh blood. I trip over a shrub and lose it. My stomach heaves, and I serve up a spectacular cocktail of bile and bad booze all over the pavement.

After a few minutes, I sense Green beside me. He hands me a white, monogrammed handkerchief, and I silently use it to clean up. That's when I realize he's holding my hair.

I look over and see Hoser's body. It's on its back a few yards away. One leg is twitching. His skull, or what's left of it, isn't.

"You knew he'd been bitten."

"I was fairly certain. And I did tell you. You didn't want my protection, so I sent you a gun."

"I'm sorry." I wipe my mouth and stand up.

"For drinking too much? For not noticing the signs of a zombie bite despite your recent education? Or for your friend over there?" He helps me stand.

All of the above, my guilty conscious answers.

I walk back into the bar and tell Pen what happened. She's too drunk to understand. I leave her on the dance floor, surrounded by men gyrating wildly. Not even a zombie apocalypse can change the fact that most guys just can't dance.

"I'm going to get drunk so that I don't have to think about anything," I tell Green. "I'm depending on you to get me home safe."

He nods but doesn't say anything.

"I'm also probably going to throw myself at you again, but I'm hoping that if I get drunk enough, I won't remember."

He nods again and smiles that maddeningly bemused smile.

I do a few more shots, Green at my side. I finally stop when my fingers start to go numb.

The rest of the evening is a messy blur, much like my lipstick after puking on the pavement outside. I remember dancing even though I don't dance. My partner looked like an angel in white jeans, white shirt, white shoes.

I'm dancing with the angel of death!

I remember the room spinning, the angel peering into my face. Then suddenly the angel uttered a single word as everything spun and faded to black.

"Fuck!"

CHAPTER FIVE

The light is too bright. I feel like I'm floating on a white cloud high in the sky. I open my eyes. I am really high -- but not in a good way -- and everything is white. *Have I died and gone to heaven?* Oh no, wait. I'm in a room with floor to ceiling windows. The headboard behind me is a giant sun. No, it's Caligula Green's beautiful face, carved into the wood like the face of Caesar.

I'm in his tower.

I'm in his bed!

With a start, I remember the evening before. The drinking. Then Hoser turning undead and trying to bite me. Then Green saving me. Then Green holding my hair as I threw up. Then more drinking, trying to forget it all.

Holy cow. Talk about a graduation party.

I peek under the covers and see that I'm completely naked. *Hmmm, did the evening get even more interesting?*

On the bedside table is a glass of juice. I taste it. It's fresh-squeezed. From actual oranges. Another first. Next to it are two painkillers; they look like the real thing, not the fake crap the druggies stamp out in their makeshift labs. I take both pills, washing them down with the juice. It's divine.

Green walks in. He's been working out and he's divine, too, his white shirt clinging to his sweaty skin and his sweat pants hanging low on his hips. *Oh my.*

Oh my god, I can see the outline of his thingy!

He opens his wardrobe and hangs the machete and baton he's carrying onto a hook inside.

"Good morning, Aurora. How are you feeling?"

"Great," I croak, then attempt a demure smile as I prop myself onto a mound of luxurious pillows. "Thanks for the juice. And the aspirin."

"My pleasure," he says, disappearing. Is he undressing in there? I try to see his naked body through the crack in the door but no dice.

"So, how did I get here?" I ask.

"The albinos," he says, poking his head around. His hair is deliciously unruly, like wild dark spaghetti. I want to eat it. "They carried you home."

"Did they undress me, too?"

"No. I did that."

I flush immediately and the blanket slips off my breasts. *Oopsie.*

"Did we...?" I can't find the words so I insert the index finger of my left hand through my closed right fist. I move my finger back and forth and waggle my eyebrows.

Green closes his eyes for a moment.

"You were unconscious," he says at last. "And necrophilia is not my thing. Not anymore." He doesn't even crack a smile. Not a wildly mysterious or slightly bemused or even a dazzling, natural, all-teeth-showing glorious kind of smile.

He's kidding, right?

I bite my lip. So, no sex. *Damn.*

"I'm sorry about last night," I tell him.

"I'm sure you are," he says. "But it was an evening I'll not soon forget." He ducks behind the closet door again. He's laughing at me, but I can't do a thing about it.

"Me neither," I say. "Except for the parts I've already forgotten." *Thank god.*

"I was able to save you, so I'm glad I was there," he says, coming out of the closet. He's still wearing his workout gear. I can smell the sweat on him. I start to get that squishy, achy feeling again.

Then I suddenly remember Hoser. The sound of the hatchet going through his skull. The blood spattering my face and clothes. The piece of his skull flying into my mouth and me quickly spitting it out. I fight a wave of nausea and sink back into the soft, white feather-filled pillows.

"How did you find me, anyway?" I say through closed eyes.

"I asked my team to keep an eye on you," he says. "I wanted to be there when the infection overwhelmed your friend."

"Team? Do you mean the albinos?"

"Yes. White draws the dead in the dark." He picks up a strange long cylinder sitting on the nightstand, taps it a few times then switches on a hidden button. I hear a low hum.

"That's why I only use albinos and only wear white," he says.

"So if I work for you, do I need to bleach my hair and skin so I'm all pale, too?" I tease.

"If you like." His expression warms a bit.

"Would that make you want me?" I sit up in bed and bite my lip.

He doesn't seem to notice so I haul out my girls and begin slowly circling the nipples with my thumbs, looking up at him demurely through my naturally thick, dark, mascara-free lashes.

"Not in the way you're hoping, Aurora," he says at last, barely glancing at me. He's still toying with the cylinder. "I'm never going to bring you flowers, not even white ones. I shut off my heart long ago. My interest is singular: survival, above all else. It keeps me alive. It keeps the city alive."

I flop back down on the bed, knees up, slowly opening and closing my legs like a drawbridge.

"I feel bad about Hoser," I say after a while.

"Why? Did you bite him?" he snaps. "Get past it, Aurora. You're alive and that's all that matters. Staying alive and staying strong."

He looks down at me with his piercing, hooded eyes. They narrow.

"Speaking of which, when's the last time you ate anything?" he asks.

I flush scarlet and turn away from him. *What's it to you? You're not the boss of me!* my inner angst-ridden teenager screams.

"I don't remember," I say at last.

Green sighs. "You need to eat, Aurora. In our world it's imperative to keep your strength up. You have to be ready to fight at any time."

"You're such a control freak," I pout.

"You have no idea," he says dryly. "I'm going to shower. You can take one after me."

Without warning, he strips and saunters into his bathroom. Unfortunately, he turns before I can get a good look at his equipment. I gape at his back muscles and his ass, though. *I'd love to fresh squeeze that.*

He's got quite a collection of scars, too, like he was used as a scratching post at some point. They must have hurt like a motherfucker but I find them incredibly hot. My medulla oblongata stops firing and my basal ganglia completely short circuits. *Oh my.*

Within seconds, a cloud comes out from under the bathroom door. Is that steam? He has *hot water! And steam!* Life is good in the tower.

A few minutes later, he comes out of the bathroom with a towel wrapped around his waist and another in his hand. He's wet.

He's not the only one.

I jump out of bed naked but he doesn't seem to notice. I stand in front of him for a moment, hoping he'll stroke my arm or brush against my breasts, but he simply pushes me to the side and opens his wardrobe. I slink into the shower. At this point, I'm as hot for it as I am for Green.

The bathroom has pristine tiles and the biggest shower head I've ever seen. As the hot water starts to caress me, it's almost as good as if it were Caligula Green's tongue. I rub soap all over my body and between my legs. I close my eyes and imagine it is his tongue. *Who needs flowers if I can get this?* My heart races. He can't be celibate. He's too hot! And he looked like he was about to lose control when he saved me. My fingers get busy.

I finish myself off within seconds. One orgasm is enough for me this morning and, like most women, I come like clockwork. Then I get even busier with the shampoo and conditioner. There's even hair gel on the counter when I'm done, but no brush or blow drier. I comb my hair out with my fingers, Caligula Green-style, then open the bathroom door and saunter into the room, sans towel.

On the bed there's a fresh set of white clothes for me. Caligula is already dressed.

"Your clothes were covered with gore and vomit," he says. "They're being cleaned." He turns on his heel and leaves the room.

I put the clothes on. They fit perfectly. And there's no underwear, so either he was paying attention to my style or his albinos weren't able to find any white underpants.

I glance at myself in the wardrobe mirror. My hair looks crazy but at least it's clean. Then I reach into my jeans pocket out of habit. I find a white hair tie. *He thinks of everything!*

I tie it back and then head out of the bedroom.

Caligula is in the kitchen when I come out of the bedroom. It's immense, of course, as is his living room. I glance around as I walk to the table, noticing his beautiful furniture, his huge collection of media, his stereo, his wall-sized TV and library. All the books and movies are about death, dying, and the undead, with the exception of a few medical textbooks. And a copy of *Green Eggs and Ham*.

He wants kids! my inner psycho chick squeaks. My inner librarian rolls her eyes. Nothing's alphabetized.

I turn a corner and realize we're not alone. Caligula is ranting to an albino who is furiously taking notes.

"You tell them they have to give me anything I want no matter how unusual it may seem," he fumes. "Canned beets! A tiny toy piano! A piñata! I can't kill the undead with my bare hands. Or burn them without accelerant. I need bullets, bulldozers, building materials! There are holes in the wall everywhere. Give them the list again. Tell them I'm not going out unarmed. And pass on my plans to expand and shore-up the southeastern wall!"

The albino nods and hurriedly leaves.

I notice the table is laden with food. It all looks great, even the canned beets, and smells even better. Amazingly, most of it is meat. There's more sausage on the table than there was dancing around Pen last night.

I stare at it for a moment, trying to remember the last time I had eggs or bacon or sausage.

"I didn't know what you liked so I had my man make multiple dishes." Caligula points to a seat.

"Very profligate of you," I say, nibbling coquettishly on a triangle of toast. He turns away to jot down some notes, and I furiously grab handfuls of bacon, scrambled eggs, and pancakes and begin wolfing them down.

I'm famished, especially after my showergasm.

"What's this?" I ask, holding up a yellow fruit, when he turns back around.

"A grapefruit." He actually smiles and begins pointing to various things. *He's laughing at me again.* "That's a clump of grapes. That's a pineapple. And these are potatoes."

"Oh, I've seen potatoes before," I say and roll my eyes.

"Yes, you do seem familiar with them," he says, wiping a chunk of hash browns off my face.

"Tea?" he asks.

"Fuck that! I mean, no thanks. But I'd love some more of that coffee."

"Trafalgar!"

An albino runs in with a steaming pot, already brewed. Caligula takes it from him and pours me a cup.

"Wow," I say, my eyes widening. "Thanks. And ... uh ... thanks for the clothes, too."

"It's my pleasure. White suits you. Especially when you blush. I love the contrast of deep red against bright white."

His eyes blaze and as if on cue, I blush. I want him to rip my white clothes off and show him just how hot and red I can get.

Breathe, Ro, breathe!

"I really should give you something for the clothes," I say, starting to get up. "In fact, I'd love to give you a blo--"

"There's really no need, Miss Foyle," Green snaps and I sit back down.

He's so mercurial!

"You don't need to bark at me," I huff. "I just wanted to be fair. I'm not working for you yet, you know."

Green looks at me, his eyes suddenly dark.

"One day, Aurora, you'll do exactly as I tell you," he says. "And more than that, you'll like it."

Control freak! Control freak! my inner therapist warns.

I nibble at my toast again, waiting for him to turn around so I can stuff more sausage into my mouth. His jaw is clenching and unclenching. I realize he's upset.

"It's just that you've given me so much," I say, my voice softening. "I'm not used to that. I'm used to taking care of myself. Of paying my own way."

He's silent but appears to be listening.

"Why did you send me that gun, Caligula?"

He looks across the table at me, his eyes burning with unfathomable emotion. Or maybe it's conjunctivitis.

"I couldn't stop thinking about the zombie that attacked you after the photo shoot," he says. "And about your friend who'd been bit. I wanted you to be able to defend yourself."

"I was too freaked out," I whisper. "I had the gun with me. But I couldn't shoot Hoser. He was my friend."

"That's why I came," he says. "To protect you. There's something about you, Aurora. Something completely irritating, yet irresistible, like a badly written BDSM novel. I'm finding it impossible to stay away."

"Then don't," I say, my teeth grazing my lower lip.

He seems shaken for a moment. "I don't think I'll be able to. I fear I'm becoming like the things I hunt."

"So you're looking for a girl with braaaaiiiiiins?" I smile.

"Something like that," he smirks.

Suddenly, he stiffens, and not in a good way. At least as far as I can tell.

"Aurora, are you going to take me up on my job offer?" He's very professional. At least until I bite my lip.

I shrug. "I don't know."

Now he looks a bit hot and bothered. Fixated. I bite my lip harder. His eyes burn with hunger.

"One of these days *I'm* going to take a bite of that lip," he says.

Oh my. I close my mouth and bite my tongue for a change.

"Will you think about it seriously? It really is the best way." My eyes hold his, then I roll them.

"You haven't even told me what you want me to do," I say. "I can't agree to work for you unless I know more."

He nods. He's back in control.

"I haven't told you because you haven't been ready to hear it," he says. "I have very special plans for you, Aurora Foyle."

Special plans? For me? My inner sex goddess starts doing her Kegels.

"What does that mean?"

"It means we need to meet again," he says, standing. "Tonight. I'll show you what I mean after you get off work. Which should be around five o'clock, if I'm not mistaken. Be ready for me by eight. And don't bother asking how I know your schedule. Just assume I know everything about you at this point, including your predilection for hair ties and going commando. Now hurry up and finish your breakfast."

"I'm full," I tell him, pushing my plate away. "And if you really want me to be your faithful sidekick, I think you should just tell me everything right now."

Green pauses dramatically and pierces me with his gaze. "You'll know tonight," he says. "Then you'll either come work for me or you'll never see me again."

What? My inner sex goddess begins wailing. *No more hot showers! No more real coffee! No more fantasies about tapping that fine ass!*

"That's it? If I don't take your job, you'll just write me off? I thought you wanted to protect me."

He sighs and steeples his long-fingered hands.

"It's not that," he says. "It's just ... Once I tell you everything, you may never want to see *me* again."

I've already seen the albinos. I know he hunts the dead and that he's a mega control freak. *How much worse could this bad boy get?*

"Can't you please tell me now?" I whisper.

"No. I have a lot of laundry to do. It takes a lot of effort to keep these whites white," he says, deadpan. "Now finish your food like a good girl."

He picks up a platter and slides the meat onto my plate then stands over me as I eat every bite. I hate being controlled but non-spoiled meat is almost impossible to come by. I just wish it was his meat in my mouth.

I stuff in the last bit of sausage, dab my mouth with a napkin, then sit back to rest for a minute, but he immediately grabs my arm and escorts me to the elevator. I'm still chewing as we start our descent. I feel like a squirrel.

Suddenly, I realize I'm about to step back into a world where my friend is dead. And undead. And then dead again.

"Oh Hoser," I say, my mouth still full. "Can't believe he's. Dead."

"Yes, Hoser," Green echoes, a strange light filling his eyes. "Killing him was such a ... pity." He suddenly turns to me and practically snarls, then pushes me up against the wall of the elevator, holding my head back like Hoser did last night.

He runs his mouth along my jawline, nibbling, and I moan despite the meat in my mouth. He brings his face up to mine and plunges his tongue in. He grabs what I'm chewing in his teeth and tears it out of my mouth, growling. I've never made out like this before. It's like French kissing a hungry dog.

My jaw feels like it's been dislocated and my legs are jelly. I'm completely helpless, but in a good way. I can feel his erection against my belly. Or maybe it's his hatchet.

We arrive at the first floor.

He swallows my sausage then gives me a greasy, yet mysterious smile.

"You. Are. So. Savory," he says. "Aurora Foyle, what am I going to do with you?"

I swallow what's left in my mouth, too. And blush furiously.

He suddenly looks hungry again.

Oh my.

"What is it about elevators?" I hear one of the albino guards whisper as Caligula Green pushes me out into the lobby. The doors close behind me, whisking him back upstairs.

CHAPTER SIX

I head for the lobby doors and make it about ten steps when I hear the ding of the elevator behind me. It's him.

"On second thought, Miss Foyle, I'll walk you home."

Outside, we turn toward Pioneer Square. I'm not sure whether he's going to pretend the elevator scene didn't happen or if he's taking me home to do me. I think I may have imagined it all. But my lip hurts and I'm a little hungry. *Did he bite it trying to get the sausage out of my mouth?*

A few blocks down the street, an albino suddenly runs up to Green. He leans in close and whispers in his ear. Green snaps.

"Tell those idiots I'll be there when I'm good and ready. I need to finish with Miss Foyle first. And I want her NDA ready when I arrive home."

Finish with me? Or finish me? And what the hell is an NDA?

"Aurora, what happened in the elevator won't happen again," he says quietly when the albino leaves.

"Oh?" I say. *Damn.* It was a little weird, but I kind of liked his version of doggie-style. "Well, I get that you were probably still hungry. That sausage was really goo--"

"I spend a lot of time with the undead," he interrupts. "I study them, I read about them, I try to get inside their heads. But it's dangerous, as I'm sure you know. *I Am Legend* and all that."

Jeez, what a conceited ass. My inner sex goddess nods eagerly. *Yes, oh yes, what an ass.*

"It's impossible to spend that much time with the undead without picking up a few of their quirks," he says. "I lost control in the elevator." He scowls. "In the future I will be certain to steel myself against your singular charms."

* * *

Pen is doing some guy on our dining room table when I get back. There's a pair of dirty overalls pooled on the floor next to a plastic jug of hand sanitizer. Zombie cleanup crew. She's on her back when I walk in, with him on top, pounding away. He doesn't miss a beat when she flips over onto her stomach so she can talk. The guy must not be very big or very good. Or maybe he's not very both.

"Hi Ro! Morning Caligula!" She shrieks a bit on that final vowel. Maybe she's having a better time than I thought. "You guys up for a four way?"

The guy licks Penelope's back as if claiming his territory. I'm used to Pen and her men. But it's a little weird that Green doesn't even seem to notice. The man lives on a completely different plane. Or planet.

"Later," he says, staring intently into my eyes. "I'll meet you here at eight." Then he steps back out the front door.

Pen's date finishes with a grunt then pulls out with a *schluck*. I can tell Pen wants to talk because she gets up, hands him his pants and points to the door. He hands her the jug of Purell and leaves, too.

"So did you?" she asks, pulling her clothes back on.

"No," I snap. "You obviously did, though. You know we eat off of that table."

She grins. "Oh I ate here."

I glare at her and she stares back.

"Hmmm, I guess you didn't do it," she finally says. "But you like him, though. I can totally tell you like him."

I can't hold the glare any longer. I smile and nod. "Yeah. We're going out tonight. But I think it's mostly to talk about that job he wants me to take."

"Man, the guy is totally obsessed with his work. So did he even kiss you?"

"Once," I murmur. "But I think he was just feeling peckish."

Pen shrugs, then suddenly grabs me by the shoulders.

"Hmmmm," she says, twisting me this way and that, examining me closely. She lets go of my shoulders and piles my hair on top of my head. Then frowns and lets it drop.

"You'll be feeling his pecker once I'm through with you," she says. "I'm going to make you irresistible for your date with the mighty zombie hunter tonight."

I go to work for a few hours then come home and eat some fresh salad (more bounty from Pen's dining table romp), then Pen and I have at it with what passes for beauty products these days. In a cold bath my roommate scrubs me all over with a washcloth, then afterward waxes off every hair below my neck and a few above it. After that, I rinse every orifice, top and bottom, with mouthwash. It stings a bit but Pen says that's how you know it's working. Then she plops me on the floor between her legs and checks my hair for lice. Once that's over, she gives me an enema and does a bit of anal bleaching. After that, she moisturizes me all over and gives me a pedicure. She even offers me her last bottle of nail polish. It's the best afternoon I've had in months.

As the hour approaches, she pours me into another one of her tight-fitting latex outfits. It feels slick against my skin, like I'm wearing a giant condom.

I kill time before my date watching zombie movies on my new iPod. The undead make me think of Hoser and what would have happened to me if Green hadn't been there. He's a control freak and one of the weirdest kissers I've ever met, but the guy is starting to grow on me. *But do I want to work for him?*

Right on time there's a knock on the door.

"Good evening, Miss Foyle," he says as I swing it open.

"Mr. Green." I nod. "Long day?"

His white coat and waterproof pants are misted with water. His shotgun is gone, but he has his hatchet. It hasn't rained so why is he damp?

"Yes, very long. I was outside the wall. The undead were threatening our northern border near the U District. Lots of zombies with hoodies and tattoos and backpacks today."

He runs a hand through his gorgeous hair. "I had them rinse off the gore at the scene so I could come straight here."

"You could have gone home and cleaned up."

He shakes his head.

"A zombie apocalypse is no excuse for being late," he says. He grabs my arm, barely registering what I'm wearing, and we begin to walk. Just as before, I feel a current running between us, only this time it seems more powerful. I can almost hear the crackling of electricity.

Breathe, Ro, breathe!

I think he's going to take me back to his building but instead, he steers me toward the water. He strides confidently ahead while I try to keep up in Pen's tottering heels.

"Can you slow down a little?" I finally ask and he does, waiting for me to catch up. As I stumble, he reaches out and grabs my elbow. I feel the electrical current again and shake my head, trying to ignore it. I look over at him and notice the remains of an eyeball dangling off the back of his collar. I try to ignore that, too, but it keeps staring at me.

I finally reach up to brush it off, and the electrical crackling goes off again. This time, there's a spark and a pop.

"Is something burning?" I ask.

He sniffs the air, then looks down at his hand. I can see more sparking.

"Sorry," he mumbles and reaches under his coat to pull out the thin cylinder I noticed earlier this morning in the bedroom. I thought it was some kind of weird dildo.

"It's my cattle prod," he says. "It's been acting up lately."

He presses the button again and the slight hum, along with the crazy current between us, dies.

Oh.

We walk under the old Alaskan Way Viaduct, which used to transport thousands of commuters between West Seattle and the city each day, and head toward the ferry terminal. It's starting to get dark, and I'm a little nervous even though the waterfront is one of the safest places in the city. The undead can't swim, although now and then one will manage to make it across the sea floor --

or float across the bay -- without falling apart or becoming fish food. The remains make for a pretty creepy low tide, but on the upside they're great snacks for the birds and the number of bones in the bay is making the sand on Seattle's beaches really soft and loamy.

The seagulls are out in full force as we approach the dock. They're bigger and much more plentiful than they used to be, probably because meat, tainted or otherwise, is a lot more nutritious than French fries. I watch as they scan the shore, waiting for a zombie to float to the surface or crawl out of the water beneath the pier so they can attack. They're like shrieking watchdogs that cover everything in shit.

Everything except for the speedboat Green leads me to, which, in the floodlights, looks immaculate.

It's small, but sleek and, like everything else the man owns, completely white. As we climb aboard, an albino hands Green a picnic basket and his shotgun. Green checks that the gun is loaded, then stows both next to the pilot's seat.

The engine roars to life. *Gas!*

"Sit." He gestures to the seat next to him. "Put this on." He hands me a life jacket. White, of course. He puts his on, then kneels and tightens the strap that goes through my legs. He's so cold he's almost clinical.

I, on the other hand, am starting to get a little hot over the fact that his hands were *down there*.

"We're going to dine on the water," he says, returning to his seat. "I hope you don't mind. The Seattle skyline is beautiful from the water."

The sea air smells clean. But I'd rather stick my nose in his hair and head south. Even if he's been fighting the undead all day, he still smells like chocolate to me.

"Don't I need a seatbelt or something?" I ask. I don't remember ever being in a boat before.

"No." He silently shakes his head, and we pull away from the dock. Over Caligula's shoulder, the albino nods at us. He looks like a mime.

I giggle. The albino smiles. *Was that a wink?*

"What a delightful sound," Green says, steering the boat through a maze of smashed ferries, capsized sailboats and tankers. I stare at one, half in the water, half out, as we motor by, picturing in my mind the horrible pandemonium that must have taken place as the virus quickly spread through the ship.

Some people think the virus came to Seattle on a cruise ship; others put the blame on the biotech labs and some evil, ironic hipster who created the zombie virus as a joke. But nobody really knows how it happened. And no one knew how far and fast it spread until it was too late.

"We'll take it slowly," Green says, inching through the dark. "I have no idea what's under the water, and I don't want to risk scuttling Grace II."

"Grace II?"

"My boat," he says. I notice a mysterious smile playing across his lips.

The sky is gray and clouded, lit by a moon we can't see. The skyscrapers are mostly dark, too, though there are a few lights here and there. Off in the distance, I see the Space Needle leaning away from the city as if it's trying to escape, the victim of an out of control airplane, a zombie attack that caused the Monorail to derail, or both. The newsletters are still hashing that one out. Ditto for whatever brought on the stupid virus.

The city is dirty and damaged and claustrophobic as hell. But to me, looking back at it now from the water, it's beautiful. It's home. And it's safe, or at least it feels safe right now.

I look over at Green. His profile is even more beautiful than the city's.

He reaches into the basket and hands me a sandwich. Then he takes one for himself.

"We're going to do a little scouting to justify using the fuel," he says.

He takes us across the bay toward Alki; I've never been to West Seattle, at least not after the virus hit, but I've heard about the hordes that congregate here. On still nights, you can sometimes hear them moaning all the way across the bay.

A few hundred feet from the beach, Caligula pulls out a huge spotlight from a compartment under the bow. He flicks a switch, sending a searing beam of light at the shore. The undead slowly begin to gather in the light, one or two at a time. A few stagger toward us, wading into the water.

"Wait, what are you doing?" I ask, suddenly feeling uneasy. "Turn that thing off. They're coming for us."

"The water's deep enough to keep us safe. You're going to have to trust me, Aurora." His voice is low.

I suddenly realize he's a man with a plan.

"You're going to kill them, aren't you?" I say. If I were here with anyone else, I'd feel sick. Terrified out of my mind. The moaning from the shore is louder now; the splashes more frequent. I keep my eyes on Green.

"Yes, I'm going to kill them," he says. "More food for the fish."

I look up and see a few dozen zombies shuffling into the water, following the beam. Just like moths, they're drawn to white. To light. I'm hypnotized by the crowds as

they shuffle forward, some missing hands, others jaw-
bones. Their clothes are matted with gore and mud, but I
still recognize business suits, fleece vests, Gortex jackets
and even a few Utilikilts. I wonder if I knew any of these
people. Then I stop myself.

They're not people. Not anymore.

"Mind if I try an experiment?" Green asks, suddenly.

I shrug. "Sure, as long as it doesn't involve landing
on the beach."

"Close your eyes."

I obey his command and suddenly, the beam of
light is on me. I keep my eyes closed but my face soon begins to heat up, both from the searchlight and a sudden hot
flush.

Oh my god, he can probably see every pore!

Even with my eyes closed and our boat 100 feet
from shore, I can hear the undead perk up. Suddenly, it
sounds like a mob is rushing into the water.

"Just as I thought," Green murmurs to himself and
the sound grows into a cacophony of loud churning
splashes and moans. It sounds like the zombies are coming
from all over to get into the water. My heart races and I feel
myself turning even deeper red. Finally, I can't take it
anymore and throw my arms up over my ears, my elbows
covering my face.

Green turns the light away.

I open my eyes, and it takes a full minute to get my
night vision back. He's shining the light at the beach again.
I look out and see an undulating shoreline. I rub my eyes
and look again. There are thousands of undead there. And
they're all coming for us.

My stomach does a flip flop. "Um, Caligula. Can we leave now?"

"By all means," he says and starts the boat on the first try. *He's so masterful!*

Within seconds, we're heading back for Seattle. But even with the loud roar of the motor, I can still hear the excited moans of the dead hoping to get at us.

I shiver a little. Green slows the boat and covers me with a blanket.

I lower my head, look up at him through my lashes. He smiles back at me. If I had a piece of sausage in my mouth right now, he might even kiss me.

Could we do it in the boat without capsizing?

"You did well tonight," he tells me.

"Thanks," I say. "It was pretty creepy seeing all of them like that, but I tried not to freak out too much."

"That's not what I meant," he says, the boat entering the downtown waters again. "The rechargeable light by itself is a good way to draw the dead into the water. It's a relatively safe and efficient way to kill them. Alone, in one night, I can usually kill a few hundred. But tonight was different."

"What do you mean?" My throat is suddenly dry.

"Didn't you notice how the dead responded when I put the light on you?" he asks me, his voice husky. "The dead want you, Aurora. They yearn for you. Instead of killing a few hundred, you just helped me kill a few thousand. In a matter of minutes."

He licks his lips, and his eyes blaze.

"You're quite something, Miss Foyle."

Oh my.

* * *

Back at the dock, Green throws the rope to an albino who secures it to the dock, then we walk back to his building.

It's fully dark now, so his attention is on the street. I know if anything comes for us, he'll take care of it.

As we approach the tower, the lights of his building suddenly go on. *All* the lights. It's spectacular, like the moon has just leapt into the sky in front of me on a clear night. And it makes all his whites look so much whiter. I have a serious case of the butterflies. Or maybe they're moths, since it's dark and they're dancing in my stomach because of the light.

"Do you always impress girls this way?"

"You're impressed?"

"I'm a little awed."

He smiles. "I'm a little odd, too."

We take the mirrored elevator up to his apartment and I surreptitiously glance at him from every angle. I'm surrounded by Caligula Green to infinity.

My inner mathematician swoons.

Within seconds, we're back in his penthouse, surrounded by white, floating high above the dark city. It's like we're in some weird science fiction movie where everyone on the ground floor wants to eat me but no one in the penthouse does.

I know he wants to talk business, but I'd rather just drink in the moment. Or drink, period.

"I don't suppose you have any alcohol," I say.

"Of course," he says. "Would white wine do?"

"Sure." *What else would he drink?*

We walk through the apartment to his kitchen, and he disappears behind the counter for a moment, then stands holding a chilled bottle and corkscrew.

He removes the cork with quick expertise. I can almost see him doing the same to a zombie's eyeball with a screwdriver. He pours the wine into two crystal goblets and offers me one.

"You're very quiet," he says, watching me. I look out at the living room.

"Do you play?" I nod toward the white piano as I suck down the wine.

"Yes. I play well. There are few things I don't do well."

I melt a little down there.

"Would you play for me?"

"Another time, perhaps," he says. "We have business to discuss."

I try to disguise my disappointment. *Always business with this one.*

"Would you like to sit?" he asks.

Yeah. On your face. My inner sex goddess is already drunk. I nod and he leads me to a couch.

"So why the quote from *Dawn of the Dead*?" I ask. My inner non-sequitur has apparently decided to join the party.

"I'm trying to get through to you, Aurora," he says. "This isn't an emotional business. You have to stay rational, logical, even if it's not your thing."

I want your thing.

"Stop biting your lip," he says, frowning. "It makes it hard to think."

I try to stop. *Not.*

"Excuse me," he says suddenly and gets up from the couch. He leaves the room for a moment, then comes back with a piece of paper.

"This is a non-disclosure agreement," he says. "An NDA. I insist you read it and sign it before we proceed any further."

No S-E-X until I sign his NDA?

"I don't understand," I say, scanning the document. It's completely full of legalese; I don't have a clue what it means. "What does it say?"

"That you'll keep my secrets. Or else."

Whatever. I grab the pen out of his hand and sign without looking at it.

"You shouldn't sign anything you haven't read, Aurora," he chides.

"You could do anything you want to me whether I sign that thing or not. Or whether I read it or not," I say. "The counsel wouldn't say anything. Not even if you took me back out to West Seattle and turned me into zombie chow. You're untouchable."

He stares at me, his eyes hooded. "Fair point, Miss Foyle."

I take another gulp of wine. Somewhere in the back of my head, I hear the hungry roar of the zombies on the beach.

"So, are you going to fuck me tonight or what?"

Shit. Did I just say that?

It doesn't even faze him.

"No, Miss Foyle, I am not," he says. "As I mentioned before, physical relationships are a distraction. I need to maintain my focus to stay alive."

A distraction? You bet your ass I'd distract you!

"I don't understand," I whine. "It's the end of the world. Who knows how long any of us will be around. Don't you want to just live for the moment? That's what everybody else is doing."

"I'm not everybody," he says. "Come, there's something I do want to show you." He stands and takes my hand.

"What is it?" I ask, eyeing his pants.

He catches my glance and shakes his head.

"It's my workshop," he says.

"You don't seem like the carpenter type to me," I say, standing and swaying just a little.

"It's not that kind of workshop."

He leads me down a hallway lined by exquisite drawings of flowers, all in black and white. Everything is quiet, muffled, like it's been sound-proofed. He gazes back at me as we reach a door and he pulls something out from under his shirt. It's a skeleton key on a heavy chain around his neck.

He takes a ragged breath, opens the door with the key, then flips on a switch. Then he stands back. I blink and totter in ahead of him.

I can feel Green close behind me, our bodies nearly touching. I know his cattle prod is turned off now, but there's still a buzz between us. Made crazier by something else. Nervousness? Restless leg syndrome?

I look around and suddenly understand why he might be nervous. It feels like I'm in a hardware store and a sex toy shop and a mad scientist's laboratory. But they're the same room.

Holy shit.

CHAPTER SEVEN

The first thing I notice is the smell. It's citrus and death with a faint trace of disinfectant.

Against one wall is a long, well-lit counter. There are a number of glass containers, test tubes, and a microscope. There's colorful liquid in several of the beakers and unlit burners here and there. Next to the counter is a refrigerator, although this one is huge. As in I could fit in there. Along with Green. And maybe a couple of albinos. Plus my inner sex goddess, and she's pretty curvaceous.

In another corner are tables made of metal, some of them fitted with deep sinks. I see a strange collection of copper tubing and glass vials that looks like something out of an old horror movie. Tools are arranged near the tables and I realize, with a start, that Green's workshop is better stocked and *way* better organized than the salvage store where I work. I see screwdrivers, wrenches, files, planes, pliers, a belt sander, and an array of saws both manual and electric, including a few so oversized and oddly-shaped that they look like they were made for giants.

It's everything I've ever seen at Elliott's and then some. Plus car batteries, an assortment of wire, a Shop-Vac. *Wait, is that a nail gun?*

Scattered among the tools are the pieces he picked up at the store the other day. I even see the plastic kid's bat.

I close my eyes for a moment, then reopen them.

In the center of the room, under another set of lights, is a comfortable-looking, red leather couch.

Hmmm. I hope it's a sleeper.

The tables and sinks gleam as if new, thanks to the carefully positioned track lighting overhead. But the corners of the room are dark. In the one closest to me, I see shackles and chains hanging from the wall. And a black zipper mask on the floor.

Is he into BDSM? Wow, still waters run deep.

I spy a cricket bat hanging from a wall hook, then identify other vaguely familiar objects hanging beside it: riding crops, rulers, whips, floggers, a badminton racquet. He *is* into BDSM.

That is so hot!

I get a sudden visual of Green bending me over his knee, spanking me with the paddle and my squishy achy place immediately turns to hot molten magma.

Unfortunately, my fantasy is rudely interrupted by a glass bureau marked "Specimens."

I move closer, as if drawn by the subtle light emanating from the case. There are a few hands in there, along with some feet, an ear, and a couple of eyeballs. And what appears to be a tongue. At least, I hope to god it's a tongue. All of the pieces are moving.

That's when I hear it. In the corner. There's a clinking. No, a rattling, like something gently tugging at a set of chains. There's moaning, too, but it's muffled. The sound is familiar.

Caligula claps twice. The lights around the sides of the room suddenly turn on.

In the far corner, I see a zombie. As the light hits it, and it sees us and registers that we see it, it begins to struggle harder against its chains. Most of its front has been torn away, leaving only a few dangling, bloated, unidentifiable organs. I can't even tell if it's male or female. It's wearing a pink rubber ball gag and its eyes are bulging. Is that a cheese grater hanging on the wall next to it?

What the fuck are you into, Caligula?

He's looking at me intently. "Say something, Aurora."

His voice is tight, strained. Although certainly not as strained as it would be if he were wearing that ball gag.

I turn to him, shocked. "A zombie? In your house!?! This is completely illegal."

I can see that the zombie isn't going to escape so I step closer.

The thing goes berserk.

I look at it, then glare at Green.

"You're putting the entire community at risk," I shout. "The undead are supposed to be killed on sight."

"Yes, I know," he says quietly. "All except the ones I keep here. For my experiments."

"Experiments?" I glance around the room at the buzz saws, the paddles, the baseball bats. "Are you some kind of sadist?"

"It's called science," he says, his voice soft but firm. From a rack of tools, he removes a pair of vice grips. He walks over to the thing chained up to the wall. He's a few feet away from it, but it's still struggling to get at me, moaning behind its gag.

Caligula adjusts the tool in his hand, recalibrating the space between the grips. He reaches up and grabs the zombie's right hand then locks the grips on one of its fingers. He pulls and cranks it sideways. The finger comes loose with a ripping sound. The zombie doesn't even notice.

Caligula looks at the finger, which is still flexing. He seems upbeat, almost happy.

"See? She didn't even notice. Nothing cruel about it. Now let's see what this finger can tell us!"

He hurries over to the counter and turns on a small burner. The little bit of green liquid in the glass container above it starts to boil. The lab smells more pleasant, like caramel corn. He drops the finger into the liquid and stares at it. It continues to move for a minute.

Oh my god, he's a scientist, too? The rumors are true! He's looking for a cure!

"Just as I thought!" he exclaims after a moment.

"What did you find?" I ask, inching closer.

"She was a married, thirty-five-year-old medical transcriptionist with two kids and a penchant for cheap chardonnay," he says. "She was beset by frequent sinus infections. She loved shoes, was a dedicated soccer mom and while she regularly attended yoga classes, she had a tendency to smoke a few Camels afterward."

"You got all of that from her finger?" I ask, amazed.

"Oh no," he says. "I used to know her."

I roll my eyes. They land on the red leather couch.

"How about if we sit for a minute," I say, nodding toward the couch. "Or better yet, have a little fun?" I waggle my eyebrows.

My inner sex goddess is panting hard despite the zombie in the corner. I try not to follow suit but I'm suddenly very turned on. I love that Green has revealed yet another aspect of his impossibly complex personality. Plus the idea of having sex while danger is mere feet away is doing something to me. Something tingly *down there.*

"You could use some of this stuff on me, too, if you're gentle," I say, gesturing to the shackles. "No pliers, though."

He turns to me and his eyes are completely intense; they're doing that hypnotic thing again.

"I'm a zombie hunter, Miss Foyle," he says. "I read about them. I watch videos of them. I train to fight them with whatever is at hand. I think about nothing but killing them. As for that ..." He gestures toward the red leather couch dismissively. "I no longer allow myself pleasures of the flesh. The only pleasure I allow myself is the pleasure of destroying the undead. And as I keep saying, I need your help."

"You seem to be doing pretty well on your own," I say dryly, looking at the parted-out medical transcriptionist in the corner.

"The hardest part of hunting zombies is finding them," he says. "They hide in the dark. Shadows within shadows. They come together in herds and then they swarm. Despite the fact that I'm in their heads and they're in mine, they remain unpredictable. Unfathomable."

He gestures to the zombie who's still trying to get at me. He's standing by it but it's completely fixated on me.

"But you," he says, hypnotically. "You could give me an edge."

"Me?" I ask, coming closer. The zombie begins to scratch at its shackles, trying to escape; it loses another finger but doesn't seem to notice.

"You're a zombie magnet, Aurora," he says. "Especially when you blush. It's your blood, your life force. It's irresistible to them. I can't be sure but I think you put off some kind of scent. Some kind of pheromone. You're like a walking, talking zombie beacon."

As if on cue, I blush deep red. The zombie goes crazy.

"Oh god, make it stop!" I cry out, trying to steady my breathing. But the harder I try to return to normal, the more scarlet I become and the more the zombie pulls at its restraints, snapping at the air.

"I don't understand," I say, backing away. I need to get out of this place. I need to hide somewhere. *Maybe inside that bottle of white wine out in the kitchen.* "How? Why?"

"I have no idea," Green says. "But I've been among them so long that I can feel it, too." He walks over to me and looks into my eyes.

Wait, what? He's drawn to me, too?

"You must stop biting your lip," he says slowly. "It's simply too much." He leans toward me, his eyes fixated on my lip. His mouth parts and he licks his lips. His beautiful, pouty lips. I tip my face up and close my eyes, waiting for his kiss. But it doesn't come. Instead, he pulls away.

I turn around, focusing my breathing. The hot flush, and my thoughts, clear. Even the zombie in the corner seems to calm down a bit. I turn around, slowly.

"So that's where I fit in? That's the so-called job you have for me? You want to use me as zombie bait."

"I want you to be my partner in killing these damned creatures," he says. "Around you, I know what they'll do. You'll be my secret weapon, Aurora. It's what I've been waiting for, hoping for."

His words cut through me like a buzz-saw. *I've been waiting and hoping for something too, Caligula.*

"I can arm you and train you so you can protect yourself, if that's what you want," he says. "I know you've received some training already. But whatever the case, I guarantee I'll kill everything that comes near you. And I also guarantee that with you on my side, everyone -- all of your friends, all of your family, all of the people living in this godforsaken city -- will be safer."

I think about his words. They're pretty inspiring. So inspiring, I realize I may just have an edge.

"And what happens after we kill the zombies?" I ask, moving closer to him. I begin twisting my hair around a finger and my teeth scrape my lower lip. "Will there be any aprés-massacre sex?"

"I, uh," he hesitates.

I'm biting my lip now and I can tell it's doing something to him.

Gotcha.

"If I become as skilled a hunter as you, could you relax a little then?" I ask. "Maybe *enjoy* yourself now and then?"

"No," he lies. "There are too many. So very, very many."

His focus is starting to waver, though. His gaze is less hypnotic and more glazed. I can see he's staring right at my plump red lip. I bite harder, wondering if I'm insane or just insanely hot for this power-mad, OCD, zombie killing freak.

The guy has a little shop of horrors in his back bedroom. He's admitted to practically being part zombie himself. But he's also incredibly powerful, a total genius, and more intense than one of his Bunsen burners set on high.

Pen said he was dangerous and boy was she right. *Dangerously hot.*

"So what would I have to do?" I ask, amazed that I'm even considering his offer.

He lets out the breath he's been holding. I can see he's starting to regain control. I let out my breath, too. It's like a dance, I realize. Back and forth, back and forth.

"First and most importantly, you'd have to learn to comply with my rules," he says. "They're for your benefit and safety. Ignore them and you'll probably get bit. The primary goal, the only goal, is not get bit in order to survive to fight another day."

"Come," he says and leads me out of the workshop, shutting the door and shutting out the sound of the chains behind him. We walk down a hall and he stops at another door, this one already open.

It's a huge bedroom with a stereo, TV, and a giant comfy-looking bed. There's also a spectacular view of Seattle through an uninterrupted floor-to-ceiling window.

Man, his window washer must get really tired.

"This would be your room," he says, nodding at the bed. "If there's anything you need, just let me know. We'll get you whatever you require. And we'll keep your whites white."

"My room?" I ask, astounded. "You want me to move in?"

"Yes. Zombie killing is a 24/7 job. The health benefits can be a little sketchy, though."

I look around the room, ignoring his attempt at a joke.

"I'd feel safer sleeping with you," I say, after a beat.

"Not an option," he says. He's fully in control now. The man in the workshop, the man who looked like he wanted to throw me down on the red leather couch and gnaw on my neck and nether regions is gone.

"Now let's get you some more food," he says. "You barely touched your sandwich earlier and you need to eat. It's nearly eleven."

He leads me back to the kitchen.

It's a mark of how well I've eaten in the last few days that I don't immediately devour the fruit and bread he puts in front of me.

"You must have questions," he says as he watches me slowly, seductively nibble on a banana. I take the whole thing in my mouth. It has zero effect.

"Ask me anything you'd like."

I give up on the banana BJ. "You said you have paperwork?"

He nods, popping a grape into his mouth. I watch him roll it around on his tongue, fantasizing about him doing the same thing to my nipples and my *special pink button*. I realize I'm drooling.

Green ignores me and goes on. "Yes, we need to figure out your hard limits so that we know what situations to avoid," he says. "If you saw your father torn apart by zombies on a grassy knoll or at a gas station or on the steps of a 1920s brick apartment building, I need to know that. We can't have you flashing back and freezing up at the wrong moment. We also need to know how many times you can swing a hammer and how far you can run in full gear. What weapon you're best with. That sort of thing."

"And if I decide *not* to take the job?"

He levels me with a cold stare. "You're a magnet for the undead, Aurora. They're going to come for you anyway. The safest thing to do is get trained, move into this building, and work with me."

"But our relationship," I roll the word around on my tongue as if it's a grape. Or one of his manly parts. "It wouldn't be strictly professional, would it?"

"You're going to be my partner," he says. "But there will be no more to it than that. No intimacy."

"I can think of few things that are more intimate," I say softly. "We'll have to have each other's backs. What's the problem with turning around and taking care of each other's fronts now and then, too?"

I bite my lip and raise my eyebrows hopefully.

"This is the only kind of relationship I'm capable of having," he says, his eyes averted. "This is who I am. Soon, it'll be who you are. That is, as soon as you sign the documents."

I lean back. *Doc-blocked again.*

"So what are these rules I have to follow?"

"I'll show you after you're done eating." Then he watches as I finish every bite. He really seems to like it when I struggle to tear the bread's tough crust apart with my teeth.

Crazy and hot. Who knew they could be such a winning combination?

When I'm done chewing, he pours me a bit more wine. Just as before, it goes straight to my head and makes me more bold.

"So how many partners have you had altogether?" I ask.

Green purses his lips.

"Ten. No, twelve," he says. He looks up as if counting. "Thirteen. Fourteen. Fifteen!" He seems embarrassed. "Sorry. In the early days, they didn't last so long."

"What happened to them?"

"Some retired. Others died foolishly and painfully. Instantly or after a long struggle against the infection."

"Did you ever have to kill any of them?"

"Of course. But only after they came back to life." He looks at me. "I'd expect you to do the same for me."

Holy shit.

"Have you ever been bitten?"

"I've been gnawed on. But I've learned the importance of the right clothing and equipment." He glances at my outfit, the one Pen spent hours putting together, for the first time. "Do you even own a pair of hiking boots? Or sneakers?" he asks, then shakes his head. "Never mind, you don't need to worry about that. I'll provide your clothing."

He reaches across the table and hands me a piece of paper. "These are the rules," he says. "As you can see, I'll provide many things for you."

I begin to read.

THE RULES:

Obedience

Do what I say when I say it or you're going to die. Or at the very least become hideously maimed. And maybe you'll put your eye out. Never hesitate. This includes training activities.

Sleep

Get as much as you can whenever you can. You never know when you're going to be on the run for days at a time. Strive for at least seven hours a night. No slumber parties. No pillow fights.

Food

All meals will be provided when you are in the building. During zombie hunting excursions, a sack lunch will be provided with your choice of fruit and beverage. Do not eat any food that is not furnished by me. I can't afford to have you ill or low on energy.

Clothes

You'll wear what I say when we're working. The clothes will fit perfectly and be color-coordinated. They will also be entirely white. And blood- and bite-proof. At all other times you will strive to look effortlessly striking. You're about to become a celebrity.

Goggles

Goggles must be worn at all times during the hunt as they keep blood from going in your eyes. When not hunting, you can wear them or let them hang rakishly around your neck. Either way, they make you look cool.

Personal items

You're going to work hard. You're going to keep everyone safe. As a result, we can get you anything you want, within reason, and sometimes stuff that's completely unreasonable. Unless you want canned beets because, apparently, we're out.

Personal Hygiene

You will shower early and often and will be allowed to use as much hot water as you like. Just because we fight the dead doesn't mean we have to smell like them.

Personal Safety
Drugs, drinking, karaoke, interpretive dancing, beer bongs, beer pong, eyeball shots, pole dancing and other questionable hobbies can impair your judgment and put both of us at risk. No alcohol, other than that provided by me and consumed in my presence, will be tolerated.

Personal Needs
The albinos can take care of your sexual needs should you require release. There are also toys available. Focus is crucial to zombie hunting. If you're distracted by desire, take care of it quickly and efficiently so you can get back to the business at hand. So to speak.

"Wait. You're telling me I'm supposed to sleep with one of the pale guys if I get horny," I ask, incredulous. "I don't want to fuck your albinos."

"They are quite skilled," he says. "But suit yourself."

"It also feels weird that we can use as many resources as we want, while everyone around us is eating squirrel burgers and making do with cold showers," I say.

He shrugs. "It's a struggle, but you'll get used to it."

My eyes return to the document. The guy has thought of everything. There's even a section on what I'm supposed to do during my period. *Oh crap, I'll be wearing white pants!*

I keep reading. Then stop when I hit a section that talks about physical training.

"Wait, I have to exercise? I hate exercise."

"Yes," he says, his lips curling into a tight smile. "You need to be strong to fight a tireless, relentless enemy. Trust me, I don't like it either. It'll be hard at first, but you'll get used to it. And speaking of hard ..."

"Yes?" I look up hopefully.

He hands me another piece of paper.

"Here are my hard limits," he says.

HARD LIMITS
Never fight zombies with fire.
Never fight zombies with gynecological instruments.
Never fight zombies with leopard stilettos.
Never fight kids on a playground.

"You'll have to respect and understand my list, just as I will with yours. Is there anything you'd like to add to that list?"

I squirm uncomfortably.

Green stares at me, his eyes penetrating deep. Unfortunately, not *that* deep.

"When you've fought the undead before, was there anything that made you hesitate?" he asks again, baring my soul with his inscrutable gaze.

I start to blush. "I ... I don't know."

"What do you mean?" His voice is suddenly as sharp as one of the band saws in his little workshop of horrors.

I shift in my seat.

"I've never done anything like this, Caligula."

"But when you were at Survival School, you killed the undead," he says. "You've been exposed to the basic methods of disposal. Was there anything that bothered you more than others? Anything you purposefully avoided?"

I blush harder. "They stopped using real zombies after the accidents a few years ago," I stammer. "After some kids died, we 'fought' our instructors who dressed up in gear and wore green makeup. They chased us around in a maze. Sometimes we'd hack at them with blunt pieces of wood. It was sort of ridiculous, actually."

"So what you're saying is ... you've never killed a zombie before?" he whispers.

I bite my lip and shake my head. I can't meet his eyes. "Never." I whisper back.

"Oh dear god, you're a virgin!"

CHAPTER EIGHT

Caligula looks like he's about to tear out two handfuls of his beautiful hair. Is he finally losing control?

"Why didn't you tell me?"

"It never came up," I reply, biting my lip. *Wow, the guy is even hotter when he's angry.*

"You were supposed to be trained," he says, his voice rising, his fingers madly raking at his unruly hair. "You live in one of the worst parts of town. The wall there is full of holes. Zombies run to you like it's summer and you're a popsicle. I knew you were inexperienced. But not *completely* inexperienced!"

He stops and stares at me, his eyes narrowing.

"Had you even seen a zombie taken out before I killed the crawler last Sunday? Or your photographer friend last night?"

"Of course. Um ... well, once or twice." *From a great distance.*

"I don't understand how you're even alive," he says, staring at me in disbelief. "I would think the undead would be sprinting toward you right and left. It's not like we've eradicated them from the city. People are still being bit."

"Why are you so mad?" I ask, indignant. I hate being treated like I'm some kind of ignorant child. Even though I try to act like one. *Men like that.* "I was taught to avoid dangerous situations. So I avoided them."

"Fuck me," Caligula sighs, his voice softening.

"I beg your pardon?" I ask hopefully.

"What I mean is, if the life I'm offering you is too much, you should just go," he says.

"I don't want to go." *I want to come.* Unfortunately, he's made it clear that's not in the cards.

"Look, it's late. It's nearly midnight." He's staring at me. "And you're biting your lip again. If you keep doing that, I'm going to chew it off."

Wait ... what? Is he trying to be funny again?

"It's not that late," I say.

He runs a long-fingered hand through his thick auburn hair. Yes, again. It's still hot.

"Come on. We need to rectify your situation right now."

Rectify? Oh my. Thank god Pen gave me that enema!

"Well, if that's what you want," I say. "I'm not really into anal, and there's usually a progression, but if you want to go directly to the dugout without rounding the bases, that's fine with me."

Caligula simply shakes his head and leads me back to the workshop. He takes out the key, gives me an intense once-over, opens the door, then turns on all the lights. The zombie in the corner once again stirs to what passes for life and starts to strain against its shackles.

"We're going to start your training tonight so that you have some idea what you're in for," he says.

"But what about your rules?"

"Fuck the rules," he says. "We can't go any further until you, well, lose your virginity. You need to kill a zombie."

He seems more engaged now, not nearly as distant.

I'm a little less into it. Killing zombies is fine in theory, but in real life, it's totally gross. Plus I feel sorry for the thing. It used to be somebody's mother.

"Maybe you can just show me some videos," I say.

He shakes his head.

"You're a brave young woman," he says, taking me by the shoulders. "And you want me to be in awe of you. You have to do this, Aurora. There's no danger. Not really."

I glance at the zombie and bite my lip.

"Except that it wants to bite that lip, too." He pauses. "It wants to bite it really hard."

I pause. Caligula is acting funny, almost as if he's turned on.

"Please, Ro, do away with this poor undead menace," he whispers, pushing me toward the tools and appliances. "Put it to rest. Use whatever you'd like. I recommend a slow thrust into its eye socket with one of these fireplace pokers."

He shivers suddenly, then reaches down and pulls the drawstring of his sweatpants. *Oh my.*

"First we have to dress the part."

He strips out of his white T-shirt and his sweat pants. Then removes his socks and his boxers. He has the most beautiful feet I've ever seen.

And that package! *Is it my birthday?*

Opening a drawer near the lab equipment, he removes two pristine, hooded white hazmat body suits. He holds one out to me.

"Well, what are you waiting for?"

I shrug and strip my clothes off as well. He gazes at me intently but I can tell he's looking at my taut muscles. (I have them even though I never work out.) He hardly glances at my magnificent breasts. Or my fine young ass.

Hello? Hot body at twelve o'clock! my inner exhibitionist screams, gesticulating wildly.

He puts our clothes in the drawer, then makes sure I've done my zipper up correctly. Gloves and footies are built into the suits. Once I'm inside the thing, he pulls a drawstring at my chin and the hood tightens around my face.

God, I must look like a giant big toe! So not hot! I try my best to keep from blushing. *I feel like such an idiot!* He takes a transparent plastic shield and affixes it to my head. It covers my entire face.

"I normally prefer goggles," he says. "But this will keep you from getting anything in your mouth if you do that open-mouthed gawping thing you so often do."

Holy mackerel. Is his package getting larger?

"I've been waiting a long time to see you do this," he says, grabbing a stray handful of hair and forcing it inside my hood. He's a little rough and my knees start to weaken. I begin to feel warm. *Down there.*

Also everywhere else.

"Do these suits breathe?" I ask.

"Yes, the Tyvek breathes," he says. "More importantly, it keeps you safe. Zombies can't bite through the material. Or claw through it. And blood and other gore easily wash off."

He continues to tuck random hairs inside my hood. I'm shaking. I do a few dozen Kegels, trying to focus.

"Can you breathe?" he asks.

I nod.

"You look good," he says.

"Thanks," I answer. "You look good, too."

"I know," he says. He always looks good. Even when he's dressed as a giant sperm.

The zombie moans around its ball gag.

"Whenever you're ready, Aurora."

I walk over to the tools. I just want to get this over with as quickly as possible. Unfortunately, I don't see Caligula's shotgun. He watches intently as I run my hands over the plastic bat, a mallet, a large screw driver.

"If you're going to use a screwdriver, I recommend the Phillips head," he says behind me. "Better traction."

I nod my head and inch toward the axes. There's a shiny, double-headed fireman's axe, a selection of hatchets, and three ice-axes of varying sizes. He must have gone "shopping" at REI. I reach for one and then another before deciding on a large axe with a hardwood handle.

It's not as heavy as the metal axes. Plus it's not sharp, so even if my swing goes awry -- and considering how clumsy I am, it probably will -- there's a better chance I won't take off my own leg.

Axe in hand, I walk over to the zombie. It's wide-eyed, even though it has no eyes. It's mostly dry, like a piece of jerky with a face, and smells more like old potatoes than bad meat. I close my eyes and take a swing. I miss and stumble to my knees.

"It's not a fucking *piñata*!" Caligula hisses. "Open your goddamn eyes."

I open them. Somehow, the thing has gotten closer. Too close. It lunges at me, teeth snapping. I look down. Some of my Tyvek sleeve is in its mouth.

"Aurora! Be careful!"

"I'm okay," I say, ripping my arm away. The thing lunges at me again; I feel its hand, nothing more than a claw now, rake against my arm, hard, and know that come morning, I'm going to have a nasty bruise. I realize this thing isn't a soccer mom any more. It's a rotting nightmare that needs to be put down.

"That's right, get your range," Caligula coaches me from behind as I step back and assess. "Take a practice swing or two."

I tee up like I'm a golfer. I'm aiming for the center of its head.

"Yes. Yes!" I glance over quickly and see that Caligula's on his knees just to my right, looking up at me through his ultra-thick, ultra-long lashes. Is his hand inside his zipper?

I turn back to the zombie and swing with all I'm worth. At the last moment, it turns and I hit the ball gag, driving it deep inside the zombie's throat. Now it's quietly gagging. I hear Caligula groan behind me.

I hit it in the head again and knock off its lower jaw. It bounces across the floor along with the straps from the gag. The thing's tongue is still moving in its face. It's lewd, like a giant worm writhing inside a corpse. As I'm watching, the ball shoots out of its esophagus and rockets across the room. A fountain of black gore sails out after the ball, spraying my mask and the front of my suit.

I clear the muck away from my visor. I looked pretty crummy before, but now I'm covered with gross zombie spunk.

Suddenly, I'm pissed.

I hit the thing's neck again. A lot. After six or seven blows, its spine is finally severed and its body hangs limply in the chains. The front of my suit is covered with blood and bits of bone and flesh. To my right, Caligula groans.

"That was fuckin' amazing," he says. "I can't believe that was your first time."

I look over at him. Despite the fact I'm covered with guts, Caligula seems to find me *hot*.

"Um, are you touching yourself?" I ask.

"I, I don't know what you mean," he says, averting his eyes.

"I can see your hand going up and down inside your suit. You're still doing it."

He looks down. And seems to notice what he's doing for the first time.

"I'd be more than happy to help you with that," I offer, grabbing a hose and turning on the water. I quickly rinse my suit off.

"I don't..." he mumbles.

"You do now," I say and grab a pair of shears from a work table. I snip the back of my suit open, between my legs. Then I cut the front of his suit open, and pull his cock out of the slit.

It's magnificent, of course.

"Wait!" he hisses, pulling a little foil packet out of the air like a magician.

"What's that? A condom?"

"Chocolate coin," he says, holding it out to me. "Your reward for a job well done."

I knock it out of his hand. *You're my reward, baby.*

"Now let's find *your* hard limit," I say, lowering myself onto him. He slides in like I'm home plate.

He squeaks and for a moment looks panicked. Then he settles in and fucks me harder than a horny marmot. It's fantastic.

"Come for me, Caligula!" I scream. "Come for me, you sick sick fuck!"

"I *am* coming, Ro!" He's quick. But he's not quicker than me.

We both explode into a million pieces -- or fifty, at the very least -- then rest and writhe and do it again. Just like before, we both come simultaneously.

It's awesome, just as I knew it would be. I'm completely spent.

"You. Are. So. Fucked. Up," he whispers to me as I begin to drift off.

"Right. Back. At. You," I answer, ecstatic and exhausted, then fall into a deep slumber.

* * *

Later, I wake up. We're both naked. And moving?

I open my eyes and realize I'm in the arms of one of the muscular albino guards. Caligula is in the arms of the other. He catches my eye as we both bounce along.

"Where?" I mumble.

"Bed," he answers. "Mine."

The albinos lay us side-by-side then quietly depart. Caligula rolls over and buries his nose in my hair.

His voice is muffled, husky. "You smell of death, Aurora."

I smile. *Thanks?*

I start to speak, but he puts a finger to my lips.

"Sleep," he whispers. "Tomorrow, I'll show you more."

I've got a few things to show you, too, I think. Then I drift off to sleep again.

CHAPTER NINE

Caligula Green is asleep next to me. He looks angelic.

Is it even legal to look that good? More to the point, is it legal to keep zombies in your apartment?

I suddenly remember his workshop. And how I killed my first zombie there. More importantly, I remember how the whole thing turned him on so much we fucked like kangaroos afterwards.

I stare into the gigantic mirror on the ceiling over his bed, admiring my perfect breasts. Then pull the covers down even further and look at my hoo hoo. I'm so sore. No surprise. I've never swung an axe in my life, and I'm not speaking euphemistically. My inner fairy godmother is tapping her foot at me. I've just entered a very dangerous world with a man who has one hell of a strange kink. *Prince Charming, he ain't.* She granted my wish and now she's trying to tell me that she can't keep me safe.

But I'm betting my fucked up white knight can and will.

I leave Caligula in bed, dress quietly, then head to the kitchen, tying my just-fucked-hair back with a white hair tie (the albinos must be keeping my pocket stocked). I'm just glad Pen isn't here to chastise me about my choices. Especially after all of my eye rolling at her laundry list of lovers.

I open the fridge and stop cold. It's like the refrigerator I used to see in my dreams, like the one I had at home with my mom back in the pre-zombie days. There's bacon and eggs and butter and cheese and milk in cold, clear bottles. There are even bins full of fresh vegetables. He must get first choice of everything growing in the gardens.

I reach in and grab an egg from a wire basket, staring at it in wonder. *Are there chickens in the city?*

Apparently, it's been too long since I've held one. The shell breaks in my hand, spilling a bit of goo on the floor. I quickly grab a bowl and drop the rest of it in.

Looks like I'm making omelets. I hope I remember how.

I'm thinking about Caligula's cock so I don't have to think about what I had to do to get access to it. I'm fixated on how well we fit together.

Just like Legos.

I grate cheese, cut up a few mushrooms and red peppers, then turn on the burner.

With a start, I notice Caligula is sitting behind me at the breakfast bar. His hair is messier than mine but still manages to look great.

"Good morning, Miss Foyle," he says.

Jesus, we're back to formalities again?

"Um, good morning. Are you hungry?" I pour the eggs into the heated omelet pan.

"Yes." He's not smiling. "We must eat. We need energy for the day ahead of us."

I continue cooking while he gets up and puts plates and silverware on the bar. After a minute, he comes over and stands behind me, tugging on my hair playfully.

I turn and put my hand to hair, gazing up at him through my lashes. *Sure, I'll play.*

He strokes my hair softly and looks deep into my eyes.

"That feels good," I tell him.

"You should consider cutting this off," he answers. "It's a bad idea to give the undead anything to hold onto."

"Oh," I say, turning back to the stove. The omelet's almost done. "Can't I just wear a hat?"

I grab the pan, cut the omelet with my spatula and put half on each of our plates. He sits down and takes a bite.

"Did you sleep well?" he asks. "I always sleep well after a killing."

I blush. "I always sleep well after I come twice."

He stares down at his plate. He seems embarrassed.

"That won't happen again." He glances up at me.

"Oh yes, it will," I say. "I've figured a few things out." I stare him down.

"Oh?"

He actually looks surprised, just like he did last night when I caught him stroking himself while I took care of Grisly Girl.

"Yes," I say. "In fact, the next time we have sex, I'd like to come three times."

"So the two of us having sex is a foregone conclusion, is it?"

"It is if you want me to follow your rules."

I bite my lip. He shifts in his seat. *Aha!*

"Eat," he says, nodding at my plate.

I take a bite, then realize how ravenous I am. Within seconds, I've inhaled the entire omelet.

Caligula is staring at his plate, but I can tell he's watching me through hooded eyes.

"You risked your life last night," he says after a moment. "You could have cut yourself with those scissors. You should have just disrobed. Never bring a sharp object near yourself when you're contaminated. Never point a blade in your own direction, period. Even a little bit of the wrong fluid in a wound can kill you and bring you back."

"I hosed off first," I say. "And you didn't seem to mind."

"There's a time and a place for everything."

"Let me tell you something," I say, leaning close. "I've been waiting my whole life for someone like you. That was the time. And that was the place."

I lean back, watching him closely. I know I'm going to have to play by his rules if I want to continue sleeping with this beautiful madman. And unfortunately, those rules involve zombies. But it doesn't mean I can't bend them a bit.

"That will never happen outside these walls," he murmurs, staring at my lip. I graze it with my teeth and he shudders.

"Of course not. But we weren't in the wild. We were in your workshop." I smile. "Next time let's try the couch."

"I don't normally have sex with my partners."

My inner fourth grader claps her hands. *I'm special!*

He pushes his empty plate away.

"Last night, your technique was sloppy," he says coldly. "Today, your training will focus on the details."

Sloppy?! Oh, wait, okay, he's talking about the zombie.

He leans in close. "Aurora, I want you to give me a head."

Head? Now we're talking!

"I'd love to," I say. "But I think Pen might be worried about me. I should probably get home. Or at least send her a message."

"Don't bother. I sent one of my men to tell her you were here." He glances at me. "She wanted details. When they weren't forthcoming, she demanded to be 'entertained.' I've never seen an albino blush before." *Was that a hint of a smile on his lips?*

We get up, leaving the dishes on the table. *How did I ever manage without an albino manservant?* He pulls out his key and we head back to the workshop.

Inside, I immediately notice the corpse in the corner is gone and everything smells freshly disinfected. The tables and couch have been rearranged and the middle of the room is now dominated by a large, clawfoot bathtub.

White, of course.

A bubble bath and oral sex? Yum! My inner sex goddess starts practicing her technique, swallowing a zucchini and then a gigantic summer sausage.

That's when I notice that the bathtub isn't empty.

Inside, wrapped tightly within a straightjacket, legs tied together with bungee cords, is a zombie. It's not gagged. As we approach -- as *I* approach -- it starts thrashing around, trying to sit up. I can tell it's trying to get at me despite the restraints.

"Mrrrrrrrrrggggggggh," it offers.

"I'm not taking a bath with that thing," I say, hugging myself and instantly reddening.

"Of course not," Caligula says, pulling off his T-shirt and then his pants. He turns to me.

"Strip," he says.

You don't have to tell me twice. In seconds, we're both completely naked.

"I don't know why the zombie has to watch but whatever," I say, moving toward him. I put one hand on his chest, the other on his man thing, then lean forward and lick his nipple. He looks down at me in horror.

"What are you doing?"

I gaze up at him through my lashes.

"Well, you said you wanted me to give you head. I thought you'd like to get in the mood first."

He sighs and is silent for a moment.

"You need to pay attention, Aurora," he says. "What I said was, I want you to give me 'a head.'"

He tosses our clothes onto the red leather couch, then crosses to the work table, grabs something, then puts it in my hand. It's a knife. The handle is black. Its thick blade is about as long as my index finger. It's wickedly sharp.

He nods at the zombie in the tub. "I want you to decapitate it with this knife," he says.

"Wait," I say. "A paring knife? Why don't you just give me a pair of nail clippers?"

"Nail clippers are time consuming," he says. "But it can be done."

"But this knife is so tiny," I protest. "Can't I just use a sword or bazooka or something."

"Yes, but that's not the point," he says. "It's imperative that you know how to dispatch the enemy. With whatever tools are at hand. You're not always going to have an armory to choose from, Aurora."

I nod. If I ever want to play ball with his balls I have to play ball.

"Now as you can see, this knife is very sharp," he says. "So you have to be careful. One slip and--"

His voice fades away, ominously.

I roll my eyes and swallow hard. *I should be swallowing him by now!*

"Remember, it can move its head," he says. "The key is to immobilize the cranium while cutting."

He makes sure I'm looking at him. "You must maintain control, Aurora."

Control, control, control. Does the guy ever think of anything else?

"Well, can I at least wear a suit, like last night?" I ask.

He hands me elbow-length gloves and a plastic apron. "You can wear these," he says. "But no suit. You need to understand that if you make a misstep, that will be the end of you. You must control your fear while you're killing."

I take a deep breath and look over at the zombie. It's wearing glasses, although one lens is cracked and the other doesn't have any glass. It looks a bit like one of my grade school teachers. *One I didn't like much.* Almost as if it senses my gaze, it begins to snap at me. It bites down so hard, one of its teeth flies out.

I inch closer to the tub, knife in my right hand. The thing growls at me and snaps its teeth again.

"Jesus!" I say, backing up.

"Focus, Aurora!" Caligula says behind me.

I inch closer, take a deep breath, then duck behind it and grab it by its wild gray hair. The zombie thrashes and the hair comes off in my hand. I back away again.

"Zombies don't respond to hair pulling," he says. "And their roots usually won't give you much leverage unless they're really fresh."

He shoves his hand into a glove, approaches, and quickly reaches out and flicks off the thing's glasses. Then he pushes his hand onto its forehead, pushing it against the back of the tub.

"This will offer you control of the head. This," he says, slowly pushing his thumb through the thing's eye and getting an even tighter grip on its forehead, "is called the bowling ball hold."

He pulls his thumb out of the zombie's eye socket. It makes a *schluck* sound.

My inner wimp groans and hides her eyes. *Ewwwwwwww.*

I step forward and shove my thumb into the hole where the zombie's eye used to be. It doesn't seem to notice, though it struggles to get free as I pin it to the side of the tub.

"Whoa, Ro," Caligula says, his eyes widening.

I take that as a good sign and push my thumb all the way in.

Even through the glove, it feels cold and wet inside the head. I pretend I'm playing in the mud. *With a knife. In a bathtub. In the nicest penthouse apartment in Seattle.*

I place the blade on the side of the zombie's neck and start cutting. It goes through the soft tissue easily.

"Christ," Caligula practically moans behind me. He really is a sick fuck.

My sick fuck, my inner psycho chick whispers adoringly.

Suddenly, it begins to struggle more fiercely, as if it's just figured out what's going on, and I stop and focus on maintaining my hold. But the deeper I cut, the slipperier it gets.

I'm suddenly reminded of the time when I was eight and I helped my mom slice up pears for a pie. They were wet and slippery and kept sliding out of my fingers onto the floor.

I push my thumb deeper into the thing's eye socket and tighten my grip on its head. Grasping the knife tighter, I push in harder, trying my best to keep my mouth shut since I don't have a mask this time.

"Oh, baby, you're doing great," Caligula says, somewhere behind me. *Is he jacking off? Again?*

I push the zombie's head against the side of the tub and keep sawing away, leaning in hard. My right hand is buried in flesh. I'm carving away but the head won't come off. Damn neck bones.

"Harder!" Caligula whispers behind me. I glance back and see that he's on his knees again and his eyes are half-closed. He looks like he's in a trance. Unfortunately, a table blocks my view of his lower half. I cut harder.

"Deeper!" Caligula whispers again, and I push the knife in further.

"Now back and forth! Back and forth!" he instructs while I saw away. I do as I'm told, trying to pretend I'm carving a ham. A bony, wiggling ham.

"Yes!" he shouts. "Yes, you're getting there. You're so close! Now thrust it in all the way. Yes, all the way! Yes! You're doing it!"

Are we talking about the same thing? I wonder as the vertebrae separate. Suddenly, the neck just comes apart, the head falls forward and the thing stops moving.

I'm completely spent but I feel victorious.

I stand up and turn around, giving Caligula a triumphant, gloating smile. His breathing is ragged, as is mine. I look down and realize my gloves and apron are completely covered with black, green and dark red gore.

"Christ, Aurora," he says, his eyes wide with astonishment. "You never cease to amaze me."

"Um, thanks," I say, picking up a hose and turning on the water. I calmly wash the gore off my gloves and remove them. I do the same for my apron.

"And you don't even have a gag reflex!" he says. "Most people would be vomiting up their breakfast after what you just did. Are you sure you've never done that before?"

"No," I say, feeling a tinge of pride.

I look down and notice a piece of spinal column in the tub. I pick it up and toss it to Caligula.

He holds it to his nose and takes a deep whiff.

"I love the smell of the undead in the morning!" he says.

I roll my eyes, and the two of us share an awkward laugh.

He's such a dork! *But he's my dork. Maybe.*

I suddenly notice his erect cock. *That could take my mind off what I just did.* I take a step toward it.

He takes a quick step back and holds up a hand, stopping me. "Not until we've been decontaminated," he says.

Suddenly the two albinos are there. They have warm, lemon-scented towels and tiny, gentle scrub brushes. They scurry around me, scrubbing me down, paying particular attention to my nails, my face and my hair. One even gives me a quick wipe or two *down there*. And then they're gone. I never take my eyes off Caligula. His erection seems to be even larger.

"You mentioned something about a gag reflex," I declare, dropping to my knees. He gasps when I go down on him. *Way down.*

He falls to his knees but I keep my mouth wrapped around him, then grab his shoulders and push him down toward the floor. I pivot and sit on his face and keep sucking away on his enormous man thing. He starts to lick my hoo hoo gently.

"That's right," I command, sitting up to fully enjoy my moment. "Get that tongue in there."

Just then, I hear a commotion from a side door, the one the albinos disappeared through a few moments ago.

There's shouting and sudden movement but it's hard to focus. Caligula's tongue is swirling around my thingamajig like the zombie goo that swirled down the workroom's drain minutes before.

"Oh, please!" I beg and the swirling and the commotion gradually increase.

I close my eyes for a minute and when I open them, I sense another presence in the room.

I look toward the door and see something shuffling toward me.

It's a woman. In a nice suit. Pearls. Lipstick. She's carrying a purse. Suddenly, I realize there's something wrong with her face.

"Mrrrrrrrrggggggggh," she says.

Just as I start to come, I realize the woman's dead.

I quickly jump up and put a table between me and this strange new undead thing. Grabbing the handiest tool, an electric reciprocating saw, I frantically start looking around for a place to plug it in.

"Shit," I hear Caligula say as he too sees the thing and jumps up. He doesn't seem as concerned, though. In fact, if anything, he seems amused.

He looks over at me, then back at the zombie, then back at me.

His eyes are wide with humored horror.

"What is that?" I ask, incredulously.

"Not what. Who," he says. "It's my mother."

CHAPTER TEN

What the fuck?

His mother is a zombie. He keeps her here in his tower and dresses her like she's going to church. And she's coming toward me now like I'm the dessert at the after-service potluck.

My eyes flick from her to him. Caligula seems unconcerned.

My inner psychoanalyst is just happy to see that his erection is disappearing.

"Don't worry," I tell him. "I've got this one."

He glances at the weapon in my hand, and his eyes widen.

"No, no. It's just my mother. I'll calm her down."

He walks around the table and gives the thing a hug. She reaches up to grab him. I see that she's wearing a Chanel suit and short white gloves.

"How are you feeling today, Mother?" he asks.

"Mmmaaaaaaahhhhhhh," it says, then begins gnawing on his shoulder.

"Good morning to you, too," he says, gently.

I quickly swap my saw for a hammer. I test its weight in my hand. *Oh my god, I'm going to have to put them both down now!* I slowly walk around the table.

Caligula turns. Instead of panicking -- *He's just been bit!* -- he's all smiles. As I get closer, I can see there isn't a mark on him. He's got one arm around her waist and her arm, holding her tight. She's straining against him, trying to rush me, but he's stronger.

His muscles are bulging. *Oh my.*

"Mom doesn't have teeth anymore," he says to me. "I even sanded down the inside of her mouth so she can't hurt anyone."

He pulls back her lip to show me and lets her gum his finger for a while.

Note to self: do not let Caligula Green do your dental work.

He finally pulls his hand away. Her lipstick is now smudged.

"Mrrrrraaaaggggggg!"

Caligula leans toward me and whispers. "Sorry. She's a little overexcited. She's never seen me with a girl before."

I start looking around for a ball gag, although I'm not sure who I want to use it on more, him or his mother. *My poor sick fucked-up fabulously wealthy beautiful man,* moons my inner psycho chick.

He reaches up with his pinky and fixes her lipstick, then stands a bit taller.

"Mother, I'd like to introduce you to Miss Aurora Foyle. Aurora, this is Grace Forest-Green."

He lets her gloved hand claw at me.

"Mrrgggaga!" she struggles.

"She says she's happy to meet you," he translates.

"Grrrsmahhhgggggg!" the thing roars and reaches for me again. I stumble back.

"What the hell?"

He smiles widely. "She says she wants you to call her Grace."

I try to smile, but my face is frozen.

"Go on," Caligula urges. "Shake her hand."

I reach out and the thing latches on. She's stronger than I expect and tries to pull me in for a good gumming.

"Nice to meet you, Grace," I say. I pull my hand away quickly, and her glove comes with it. I look down and one of her fingers is missing, along with a few nails. I feel the glove. The finger is still inside.

Hey, things could be worse, my inner absurdist says with a shrug. *At least she's not freaking out that the two of you are naked.*

I look over as the albinos file in and stand quietly behind Caligula. They don't seem to notice my fabulously nubile breasts and tight young ass, either, but then they've already seen me naked more times than they've seen me clothed. They bookend his mother and lead her gently but firmly toward the side door. One of them -- Trafalgar? -- looks at me expectantly, and I throw him the glove.

Do they dress her? Put on her makeup? Do her hair? A more horrific thought strikes me. *Or does Caligula?*

He watches the door shut, almost wistfully, then grabs his clothes from the red leather couch. I do the same, and we silently get dressed.

"Was that part of my training, too?" I ask, pulling on my pants.

"No. My family is part of my life," he says. "And if you're going to be part of it, too, you need to get to know them."

He wants me to be part of his life?! My inner school-girl starts clapping her hands again.

One of the albinos re-enters the room and Caligula walks over to him. They begin talking business, the tall, pale man speaking quietly, but urgently. For the first time, I notice a soul patch.

"They're massing at Boeing Field? Cancel my after-noon patrol," Caligula snaps. "I'll drop in behind them and take care of it. Prepare my equipment."

The albino nods and leaves.

"Is there an emergency? Do you need to go?" I ask.

"Yes and yes. But I'm going to take my time getting there. It reminds everyone about how much they need me."

He leads me back to his room, and I watch as he puts on three layers of thick, protective clothing. His stylish goggles are strapped to his forehead, mussing up his already perfectly mussed-up hair. As usual, everything down to and including his leather boots is white.

He pulls out a parka but instead of donning it, folds it into a tight square. Then out of nowhere -- *I swear I snooped through his entire closet while he was asleep* -- he pulls out a black leather jacket. It's old-school cool with a shiny silver zipper.

"I thought you always wore white." I giggle as he puts it on.

"Not when I ride," he says. He zips it up and grins at me.

I bite my lip and move closer. *Ride? Is he going to ride me before he leaves?*

The answer is no. He leads me to the elevator, and we descend to the basement without so much as a quick hand job.

Am I losing my touch?

We get out, and I'm awestruck in front of a fleet of new-looking cars, truck, and, *oh my god, is that a Hummer*?

Caligula ignores them all and instead turns to a sleek, black motorcycle tucked beside an Audi R8 Spyder. Or maybe it's a Volkswagen. I was never very good with cars. Two helmets, both gleaming white, are resting on its seat.

"Put this on," he says, handing the smaller one to me. I strap it on eagerly, excited about my first motorcycle ride.

Even though they're fast and maneuverable, gas rationing makes them unavailable to most people. But Caligula Green isn't most people. I'd seen members of the ruling counsel using them now and then but their bikes weren't anything like this. This one is shiny and black and polished and looks like something Batman would ride.

Moving closer, I notice storage bins on each side of the bike. The left side is open and is loaded with neatly organized weapons, so Caligula can pull them out as he drives. On the right side, a small picnic basket is tucked into the bin. Caligula puts his folded parka under the basket then clamps down the lid.

"Have to make sure the food doesn't fall off during our ride," he says, with a smile, then leans toward me and tightens the helmet strap below my chin.

He pulls his goggles over his eyes, straps on his helmet and climbs on the bike. I climb on behind him. As he starts it up, the engine rumbles loudly and my seat begins to vibrate *way down there.*

My nether regions tingle as we roar out of the tower's garage and out into the cluttered streets. I hold tighter to his black leather jacket, thinking of the incredible power between my legs and the incredible power that he holds. The tingling increases.

Oh my.

Oh mine! My life suddenly seems wonderful as we head out into the bright Seattle May morning.

On the streets, people turn to stare and shout about gas rationing and bike lanes -- same old Seattleites -- as we rumble by but Caligula is oblivious. His attention is on weaving in and out of the bike traffic and potholes, staying on a smooth path as we travel north. Now and then, he goes up on the sidewalk or across a dry patch of grass, scattering citizens like bowling pins. But even they seem so overcome by the vision of us and the bike, poetry in black and white, that they don't even bother shouting. They just throw things.

Confetti? Flowers? Refuse? It's hard to say.

I'm lost in thought but suddenly realize Caligula isn't driving me home at all. And he isn't heading toward Boeing Field either. I don't know where he's going but I feel the wind against my face and the bugs in my teeth and I realize that I don't care. I don't care about the zombies. I don't care about hiding out in my safe little apartment. For the first time in years, I feel alive.

We wend our way through Belltown and then Uptown until we're finally heading up Queen Anne Hill. Its streets are filled with years-old traffic and the occasional dried-out corpse. My mother lives on the other side of the hill, near the northern border. *Two moms in one day?*

"Hold on," he shouts as the bike rolls over a body and keeps climbing. At the top of the hill, he takes a sharp left, then slows. He stops at what used to be a park, a place where tourists used to come to take pictures of the city.

He parks the bike near a sign, now bent and rusted. Kerry Park, it reads, although someone has spray-painted an "S" in front of the "K". I hop off and walk toward the lookout.

Back in the day, the view here used to be spectacular: skyscrapers, Elliott Bay and its ferries and ships, Mt. Rainier in the distance.

I can still see the mountain, but now the ferries are capsized or listing, the Space Needle is tilted at a sad angle, and many buildings are simply gone, lost to fire or brought down years ago in order to kill off nesting zombie hordes.

Seattle is a wasteland, although here, on this gorgeous sunny Sunday morning with Caligula, it's *our* beautiful wasteland.

We sit in a weedy patch of grass at the edge of a vegetable garden. Like every other park in the city, what was once lawn or sports field or playground has been converted into urban farmland. Below me, I watch as a handful of workers push small starts into the ground. Planting season. One of the workers, a woman, gets up and heads toward a flat, rubbing her back.

That'll be me in a few weeks unless I decide to go the junior zombie hunter route.

"I had the albinos pack a lunch," Caligula says, grabbing the basket off the bike. "I thought you might be hungry after your big morning."

I flash back on the decapitated body in the tub, the meeting with his "mombie."

He sets the basket down between us, then takes out a thermos and two plastic mugs.

"Nettle soup," he says, opening a thermos and pouring a gloppy light green liquid into the cups. I take a tentative sip. My lip feels a little numb but it's delicious.

Caligula nods approvingly as I take another sip, then reaches in the basket again and pulls out a loaf of bread and some sausages.

"You seem to really like sausages," I say, wondering if my fucked up fabulous man might be the teensiest bit latent.

"They keep longer than most meat," he says, pulling out a knife and slitting my loaf apart.

Oh my.

He hands it to me then grabs a sausage for himself and bites the tip.

My mouth pops open.

"Put that thing in your mouth, Aurora," he says.

I instantly flush. *Oh boy, Oberto!*

I slide my sausage into the splayed bread loaf then take a small bite, watching him.

He's staring off at the water and in this light, his eyes look blue. Mine, on the other hand, feel like they're full of bugs.

I don't even want to think about my hair.

Helmet head! Helmet head! my inner bully taunts.

"You have a really nice bike," I say after a while.

He smiles and turns back to me. I see something in his eyes. A cloudiness. Sadness? The early stages of glaucoma?

"My mother really liked you," he says at last.

Your mother would really like anyone who was breathing.

"That's nice," I say, wondering, exactly, how to word my next question.

"She's never met any of my partners before," he murmurs.

But has she eaten any of them?

"Have you ever thought about … letting her go?"

"No. When she was turning, I made a promise to her that things would get better. So I try to make sure they're a little better every day."

He is trying to cure them. Because he wants to cure his mother!

"Why didn't you introduce your other partners to her?" I ask. "Were you afraid she'd hurt them?"

"Quite the opposite," he says. "They tried to stand in my way. Which is why I was glad to see you two getting along so well."

"What did they do?"

"Tried to make me put her down," he says, looking away. He frowns for a moment, engaged in some deep internal struggle.

Hmmm, maybe sausages don't keep that long.

"My first partner was the most adamant about it, which is odd because she was a friend of my mother's," he says at last. "We ... worked together, when the world first changed."

I sense there's more to the story and take a ragged breath.

"You worked together or you banged her?" I say.

Caligula looks at me. His eyes turn a steely gray.

"Of course I banged her," he says. "I was a teenager. I was all hormones. And the world was coming apart at the seams. What else could we do?"

"So you were humping some old lady?"

The thought of him in bed with a woman in her, -- what, 30s, 40s, *50s?* -- totally creeps me out.

"Yes, I was humping her," he says, shrugging. "When we weren't barricading ourselves inside my mother's house or out hunting supplies. She taught me many things."

It suddenly feels like he's reminiscing. And I feel like throwing up.

"So how old was she?" I ask, horrified. I know I'm obsessing but I just can't get past the age thing.

My beautiful man in the arms of ... the Crypt Keeper!

He shrugs again. "What does it matter?" he asks. "Age is relative."

"Your mother is a relative," I say, suddenly wondering if he might have fucked her, too. *Maybe that's why he didn't want to do you,* my subconscious whispers. *He can only get off on old women!*

Caligula shakes his head, takes a deep breath, then silently bites into his sandwich. I try to do the same, but I've lost my appetite.

I try to get back to on track.

"So you two hunted zombies together?" I ask.

He nods slowly and his eyes get all misty. *Oh no, here we go again!*

"The first time we had sex was right after our first zombie kill," he says. "Her husband. I was over at their house, mowing their lawn. He'd been bitten, but she didn't know. We were too inexperienced to read the signs."

I'm silent, heart pounding, lip unchewed.

"I took him out with a pair of electric clippers." He shrugs. "She didn't love him anymore anyway."

I flash on the hand back at his office, the one with the tasteful placard. First kill. *First thrill?*

"I don't need to hear any more about the sex," I say. "I get it. You fucked your mother's friend."

"The last time we had sex was after *she'd* been bitten," he continues. "I thought she was just ill. Back then, people still got viruses. She knew she was dying, though. She made me promise to kill her if she came back."

His voice catches and I look at his face. It's grim, as if he's reliving the moment. I bite my lip and suddenly I'm reliving my sandwich.

"I told her she was being overly dramatic, that she just had the flu," he says. "And then I made love to her. She was groaning and sweating and then became still. I thought she'd come. But suddenly, she was groaning again and trying, literally, to tear me apart. I can still feel the coldness surrounding my ..." He pauses and looks down.

I grimace. *Wait -- he didn't just fuck an old lady? He fucked a zombie?*

"Somehow, I managed to grab the handcuffs from the nightstand and restrain her, then I shoved her purple dildo down her throat."

He pauses, takes a ragged breath.

"And then?"

"And then I stabbed her to death with one of the leopard stilettos I was wearing," he says.

He looks out across the water. It twinkles in the sunlight, like the diamonds on his mother's tasteful earrings.

Wait. He wore leopard stilettos to bed? My inner sex goddess makes a mental note to check out his closet.

"I'm lucky she had peculiar tastes," he says, after a minute. "I'm only alive because she was a little kinky."

He suddenly turns and locks eyes with me.

"After that, I vowed never to mix sex and survival again," he says. "But now I've broken that vow. Thanks to you, Aurora."

That's right, baby! You're mine now! My inner heel does a butt-shaking dance of victory. But I'm still freaked out that he was with someone his mother's age.

What if he prefers old ladies? my subconscious hammers away at me. *You're young and hot. You can't compete with crow's feet and varicose veins!*

"Aurora, I know what I'm asking is difficult, but I really want to make this work," he says, his eyes burning with sincerity. "In fact, I've never wanted anything as much as I want this. You have something special. Something I've never seen before. The two of us--"

"Yes?" I ask, gazing at him longingly.

"The two of us may be able to completely wipe out these godforsaken creatures," he says. "We can expand the walls and bring more survivors to safety. We can rebuild society."

"And then?" I ask, hopefully. *We can live happily ever after in your fabulous tower castle?* my fairy godmother fills in the blank.

"And then we can do the same for other cities," he says. "I know there must be other strongholds out there."

He grabs my hands, squeezes them tight.

"I'm going to send you an employment contract that outlines everything," he says. "Read it, think about it, and get back to me with any questions you might have. This is huge, Aurora. Our entire society may rely on it. On you."

I bite my lip and nod.

"Okay," I say. "It's a big step. But I'll think about it."

* * *

We finish the rest of our picnic in silence. Ditto for the ride back to my place. I'm completely exhausted and still reeling from his disclosure and my day. *Zombies, mombies, cougars and that weird nettle soup.* I hug his back tightly as we ride, letting him know he's not alone.

It's just after three when he pulls in front of my place.

"Stay safe," he tells me, handing me a small axe from his weapons cache. There's a lump in my throat, and this time it's not sausage.

I watch wistfully as he roars off to take care of the emergency. If there's still even an emergency. Caligula Green, you are one complicated, self-obsessed, fucked up man.

I scurry into the house with my axe, and jump as I see Pen suddenly come around a corner, her face tinged with green.

Oh my god, she's been bit! How? When!?

I raise my axe, ready to off her.

"Whoa, Ro! What the hell?" she shouts, and I slowly lower the handle.

"Your face," I say, reaching up to touch her skin. A bit of the green flakes off. She's wearing a mudpack. "You looked dead."

"It's Clinique," she says, grinning. The green mud cracks and more flakes off. "A team finally made it all the way to Southcenter Mall! And you don't want to know who I had to fuck to get these skin care products."

I shake my head and try to walk around her but she won't have it.

"Looks like you've been doing a little training," she says, blocking my way. "I hope you got some extra-credit, too."

"I'm the teacher's pet," I say, pushing past her. "And he's my pet, too."

She raises her eyebrows and turns to watch me walk toward my room.

"Are you limping?"

I stop and turn around. "Yeah, I'm a little sore."

"You kill one of them?"

I nod and hold up two fingers. "Decapitation."

Pens lifts her eyebrows. I can tell she's impressed.

"My first time was horrid," she says. "It was on the couch in my mother's basement. The TV remote was digging into in my back the whole time. Until I pushed it through his eye."

"The first one wasn't too bad," I tell her. "But the second one was pretty intense." She wants more, but I'm too tired.

"Hoser's funeral is Friday night," she says as I inch toward my room. "We're having it at what was supposed to be his gallery. I hope you can make it."

"Of course." I duck into my room and turn on my new media player, trying to focus on *The Omega Man*.

Instead I start thinking about Caligula. Talk about a godforsaken creature. He was banging some old lady when she turned. He's got illegal zombies in his tower -- including his own mother. And he refuses to allow himself any pleasures of the flesh. Sure, he's powerful, self-assured, arrogant and super hot, but he also can't get it up unless zombies are involved.

I'm sure Dr. Freud would have had a field day with that.

But he's also gorgeous, young, smart and built like a brick shithouse, my inner sex goddess reminds me. *Plus he's trying to save the world.*

He also seems to be willing to give me what I want. As long as I agree to be bait. Which means going outside the walls. It's a big step, and I'm not sure I'm ready for it.

I masturbate a little to help me think about it. Then I drift off.

CHAPTER ELEVEN

I wake up. One of the albinos is in my room, standing by my bed. He's looking at me, but he's not staring even though I'm naked and have kicked the covers off. It's sort of like being watched by a big white cat.

As soon as my eyes open, he hands me a manila envelope then leaves as quietly as he came in. I wonder for a moment if Pen let him in or if he found his own way past our locks and barricades. I decide I'd rather not know.

I sit up groggily. *Working for coffee might not be such a bad idea.* Tearing the envelope open, I find the promised employment contract inside.

I begin to read.

CONTRACT
Made this day _____ of 2012 between

Mr. Caligula Green of the cleanest, shiniest, fanciest building in Seattle, WA
("Master Zombie Hunter")

Miss Aurora Foyle of a basement hovel in Pioneer Square, Seattle, WA
("The Bait")

THE PARTIES AGREE TO THE FOLLOWING

FUNDAMENTAL TERMS

1 The purpose of this relationship is the elimination of the undead in and around what's left of Seattle.

2 The Bait and the Master Zombie Hunter agree that their safety is of paramount importance. If they're not safe, the city is not safe. Both agree to follow all safety procedures set out in the contract.

3 The Bait and the Master Zombie Hunter warrant that they're in good physical health and suffer from no diseases or injuries, with the exception of a few carpet burns, a possible urinary tract infection and a slightly gnawed lip.

4 The Bait and the Master Zombie Hunter each authorize the other to eliminate him or her in the event of imminent zombification through viral infection.

ROLES

5 The Master Zombie Hunter assumes responsibility for the well-being of the Bait. He shall offer training and guidance and shall plan all operations inside and outside of Seattle's walls.

6 If at any time the Master Zombie Hunter fails to follow the agreed upon terms, limitations, and safety procedures in this contract, the Bait can leave the service of the Master Zombie Hunter without notice. A note would be nice, though. Or maybe flowers.

7 The Bait must obey the Master Zombie Hunter at all times, without hesitation.

8 The Bait will be provided with housing, sustenance, and everything she could reasonably expect (and even some things she might not expect) in a post-apocalyptic society. Except for canned beets. The Bait's life will be good.

COMMENCEMENT AND TERM
9 This contract is effective for three months from the Commencement Date. At that time either party may propose an extension of the contract after a renegotiation of terms, if desired.

AVAILABILITY
10 The Bait will be available all the time. Period. The middle of the night. The middle of dinner. The middle of "business." One never knows when the undead might come calling. No one expects the Zombie Inquisition.

11 The Master Zombie Hunter reserves the right to fire the Bait at any time, for any reason. However, the Bait cannot quit without the notice and approval of the Master Zombie Hunter. Yes, he is that arrogant and demanding.

TRANSPORTATION
12 The Bait will be transported where she's needed when she's needed in rock star style. People will turn and stare. She'll be the envy of everyone who sees her. As a result, the Bait will frequently be asked to "do something with that hair."

SERVICE PROVISIONS

13 Shit happens. This contract cannot anticipate or cover all possible scenarios. The Master Zombie Hunter agrees to do his best by the Bait in all circumstances. Amendments can be proposed and agreed upon. The goal of the parties herein is to kill the undead, live through the experience, and possibly rebuild the entire human race. But no pressure.

MASTER ZOMBIE HUNTER

13.1 The Master Zombie Hunter will make the Bait's health and safety his priority. He will not allow the Bait to participate in activities unless she's properly equipped and the activities seem, in his estimation, survivable.

13.2 The Master Zombie Hunter assumes control of the Bait for the term of this contract.

13.3 The Master Zombie Hunter will provide the Bait with necessary training, orders, weapons, protective clothing, and suitably pale servants.

13.4 The Bait shall do her best to perform her duties, do as she's told, refrain from rolling her eyes an excessive amount, refrain from rolling zombie eyes an excessive amount, refrain from biting her own lip off, kill anything that shouldn't be moving and basically stay the fuck alive.

13.5 This includes activities which are exceedingly gross, exceedingly violent, exceedingly excessive and exceedingly nonsensical. Case in point, that whole bathtub scene.

13.6 All of these precautions have been set in place to make sure The Bait is not bit or otherwise infected. Really. Stop rolling your eyes.

13.7 If the Bait is injured during the course of these activities, she shall be provided medical attention. Not necessarily by a doctor -- the Master Zombie Hunter is still trying to replace his last personal physician -- but at least by one of the albinos who worked as an extra on *Grey's Anatomy*.

13.8 If The Bait is infected and about to undergo zombification, she will, of course, be killed. The Bait will have a choice, though, as to her method of elimination. As long as it does not interfere with the Master Zombie Hunter's hard limits.

13.9 The Master Zombie Hunter shall maintain his own health and safety as part of the effort to keep the Bait safe.

13.10 The Master Zombie Hunter may need to tie up or shackle or cage the Bait as part of an operation. The Master Zombie Hunter may also need to stuff a gag in the Bait's mouth at certain times. Or dose her with chloroform at certain other times to induce unconsciousness (especially if the Bait is talking too much and the Master Zombie Hunter is exhausted from a long day of killing zombies). This will only be done to keep the Bait safe. Really.

13.11 The Master Zombie Hunter's minions will attend to both the Bait and the Master Zombie Hunter's personal hygiene following each hunt. The same goes for the clean-up of tools, weapons, protective garments, goggles, clothing, accessories, hair ties, etc.

BAIT

13.12 The Bait accepts the excellence and superiority of the Master Zombie Hunter when dealing with the undead. She agrees to accept his direction and his authority.

13.13 The Bait shall obey the rules (see Appendix 1).

13.14 The Bait shall do whatever the Master Zombie Hunter says is necessary, to the best of her ability, including blushing on command.

13.15 The Bait shall maintain her health and physical fitness.

13.16 The Bait shall not touch the undead in the Workshop without permission. Especially *down there.*

13.17 The Bait shall continue to engage the Master Zombie Hunter in sexual congress. Especially after zombie hunts. He really likes it. He just has a hard time saying it.

13.18 The Bait shall do her best not to distract the Master Zombie Hunter *during* a zombie hunt or other operation with inane chatter, hair flipping, lip biting, eye rolling, teeth sucking, toe tapping, excessive squirming, excessive panting, heavy sighing, heavy petting, pulling her pants away from her buttocks or gaping at him with her mouth open. The Bait will especially not try to distract the Master Zombie Hunter during a zombie hunt by trying to seduce him. Again, he really does enjoy the sex, but it could get them both killed.

13.19 The Bait shall not mock the Master Zombie Hunter's wardrobe. Words hurt.

13.20 The Bait shall not try to kill zombies without the Master Zombie Hunter's express permission.

ACTIVITIES

14 The Bait will participate in any and all missions and training activities the Master Zombie Hunter feels are worth the effort and deems survivable. Or even missions and training activities that the Master Zombie Hunter feels like putting The Bait through because he wants to teach her a lesson or because he's in an exceptionally bad mood. No exceptions.

15 The Bait and the Master Zombie Hunter have discussed the specific activities in Appendix 3 and recorded their agreement and understanding about them.

SAFEWORDS

16 The Master Zombie Hunter and the Bait realize that zombie removal missions will not always be completed without physical and emotional harm.

17 The safeword "Shit, you've gotta be kidding me?" will be used to let the Master Zombie Hunter know that the Bait is nearing her limit of endurance. The Master Zombie Hunter promises to start focusing on a way to bring the mission to a quick close once these words are uttered.

18 The safeword "Fuck you, asshole! You're on your own!" will be used to let the Master Zombie Hunter know that the Bait has exceeded her limit and can participate no further. The Master Zombie Hunter will cease the mission as quickly as is humanly (or inhumanly) possible.

CONCLUSION
19 We the undersigned read the contract and we get it.

We accept the terms by signing below.

_____ Date _____
The Master Zombie Hunter: Caligula Green

_____ Date _____

The Bait: Aurora Foyle

APPENDIX 1: RULES

(Flip back to Chapter 7 if you really need to read these again. What kind of book would print these twice? Or three times?)

(On second thought, here it is. It helps pad the page count.)

THE RULES:

Obedience
Do what I say when I say it or you're going to die. Or at the very least become hideously maimed. And maybe you'll put your eye out. Never hesitate. This includes training activities.

Sleep
Get as much as you can whenever you can. You never know when you're going to be on the run for days at a time. Strive for at least seven hours a night. No slumber parties. No pillow fights.

Food
All meals will be provided when you are in the building. During zombie hunting excursions, a sack lunch will be provided with your choice of fruit and beverage. Do not eat any food that is not furnished by me. I can't afford to have you ill or low on energy.

Clothes
You'll wear what I say when we're working. The clothes will fit perfectly and be color-coordinated. They will also be entirely white. And blood- and bite-proof. At all other times you will strive to look effortlessly striking. You're about to become a celebrity.

Goggles
Goggles must be worn at all times during the hunt as they keep blood from going in your eyes. When not hunting, you can wear them or let them hang rakishly around your neck. Either way, they make you look cool.

Personal items
You're going to work hard. You're going to keep everyone safe. As a result, we can get you anything you want, within reason, and sometimes stuff that's completely unreasonable. Unless you want canned beets because, apparently, we're out.

Personal Hygiene
You will shower early and often and will be allowed to use as much hot water as you like. Just

because we fight the dead doesn't mean we have to smell like them.

Personal Safety

Drugs, drinking, karaoke, interpretive dancing, beer bongs, beer pong, eyeball shots, pole dancing and other questionable hobbies can impair your judgment and put both of us at risk. No alcohol, other than that provided by me and consumed in my presence, will be tolerated.

Personal Needs

~~The albinos can take care of your sexual needs should you require release. There are also toys available. Focus is crucial to zombie hunting. If you're distracted by desire, take care of it quickly and efficiently so you can get back to the business at hand. So to speak.~~ The Master Zombie Hunter is now on the job.

APPENDIX 2: HARD LIMITS

Never fight zombies with fire.

Never fight zombies with gynecological instruments.

Never fight zombies with leopard stilettos.

Never fight kids on a playground.

APPENDIX 3: SOFT LIMITS

To be discussed and agreed upon:

Which of the following is unacceptable to the Bait?
Cage
Cage suspended from a crane
Shark cage
Cage match
Black gold
Texas tea
Swimming pools
Movies stars
High diving platform
Dolphins
Anal fisting
Chains
Being chained to the wall
Burning hair (other)
Burning hair (Bait's)
Transparent plastic rain clothes
Protective clothing that's not color-coordinated

Would the Bait ever eat a dead person?

Would the Bait ever use a sex toy on the Master Zombie Hunter?

Would the Bait then consider killing a zombie with said sex toy(s)?

Can the Bait imagine how much fun this is all going to be?

Holy fuck!

I let the contract slip out of my hands. My head is all abuzz. Shark tank? Swimming pool? Sexual congress?

I don't remember that particular branch of the government.

I shake my head. This guy has thought of everything and then some. Sure, I'll try to do something about my hair. And my lip biting. I roll my eyes at the thought.

And yes, that, too.

But there's no way I'm going to eat a dead person, no matter how bad things get. Also, I hate that I have to wear white all the time. *It's so not my color.* Luckily the contract doesn't say he can bleach my hair. I bite my lip, furtively looking around. But it doesn't say that he can't, either.

Has he ever killed a zombie by fisting it? How weird would that be? I guess the situations he finds himself in really do call for unique solutions. And what's with all that stuff about being chained up or suspended from a crane or setting my hair on fire?

I shrug. *Who knows? Who cares.* I'm still reeling from the most important revelation of all: *He's into me!*

My inner goddess is doing fist pumps in the air. Or maybe she's practicing her anal fisting. *Who can say?*

I get dressed and brush my teeth. It's been a few days. Then I carry the contract out to the dining room and sit at the table staring at it.

I know Caligula is fucked up. Who isn't, with the dead walking around and eating all of our friends and family? But he's particularly troubled. He's seen his entire family turned into zombies. He's had to kill thousands of the undead with his bare hands. All right, he probably wore gloves and used weapons. The poor man's even had to have sex with someone who shopped at Coldwater Creek.

But he's hot and his hair always looks good and his package is spectacular. Plus he's got the best apartment in the city and all the food I could ever hope to eat. Except beets.

Maybe the bait thing is bullshit, something he tells all the girls. Maybe he just plays hard to get in order to get what he wants. Maybe he's just like every other commitment-phobic fuck out there.

But he smells gooooood! And his ass is so fine! My inner goddess is kneading her breasts like a sex-crazed baker.

The truth is, I want to do him. The problem is, I don't want to die.

Maybe he can arrange for better care for Mom, my inner negotiator speaks up, and I purse my lips, considering. He did say he would provide for me. And mine.

I make a mental note to ask him if Mom can come and move into the tower.

Scratch that. Maybe he can move her to Belltown.

I scan through the contract again, my brows furrowing as I read. I suppose it doesn't matter whether I go with him or not; the dead are going to get me anyway. They're going to get us all.

But maybe I can do some good before they take me out, my inner idealist whispers. *Maybe, just maybe, I can live to see my thirties.*

My inner rebel-without-a-cause bristles. *Wait, do I even* want *to live to thirty?*

I quit reading and stare at the first page. Aurora Foyle, hereafter referred to as "The Bait."

Am I bait? I guess so. I toss my hair and put on my pouty lip face. Bait comes with barbed hooks, though, so Caligula had better watch out.

I wander back to my bedroom and lie down again. I'm still sore from the weekend's antics. Before long, my eyes close and I start to doze.

I dream that I'm on a giant fish hook. Sometimes I'm sitting on it alluringly. Other times I'm dying, the sharp hook shoved through my guts. In both dreams Caligula is trying to hold himself back.

I wake to Pen's voice. "There's a man with a delivery for you."

"Wha-?"

"Come on!" She pulls me out of bed.

It's the big albino again. Trafalgar. Or the other one with the socks and sandals. They're starting to blur together. He's standing in my living room with a gigantic box. It's peppered with breathing holes and seems to be making weird noises.

I flash on Caligula's "specimens" cabinet and picture a box full of squirming tongues, fingers and eyeballs.

Suddenly, something sticks its head out of one of the holes and I jump.

"Birdies!" Pen says.

The albino silently takes a bag of birdseed from his backpack, along with a sheath of papers. He then pulls a pigeon out of the box, removes a small slip of paper from a holder on its leg and hands it to me.

There's a note scrawled across it.

To: Miss Aurora Foyle

Finally figured out a way to send you messages. Now I don't have to walk to your apartment every time I want to talk.

Caligula Green
Zombie Hunter Extraordinaire

There's a little skull above the "i" in his signature. *That's so adorable!* my inner psycho chick gushes.

But I'm confused. *Why is he being so formal, signing his note with his full name and even his frigging job title? Like I'm going to get him confused with all the* other *Caligulas in town? And why was his note specifically addressed to me? Does he have pigeons flying back and forth to other people? Other women?*

The albino gestures at me, and I follow him outside. Next to our front door is a wire-and-wood coop for the birds. He opens the box with the breathing holes and transfers half a dozen pigeons into their new home. I notice a little bell in the coop, but none of the birds are playing with it. There's also a door that allows them to come in. It's fixed so it doesn't let them out.

"So the pigeons will take messages back and forth?"

"They will."

"I thought this only worked one-way."

"These pigeons go both ways." The albino smiles. Or maybe he grimaces. He leaves shortly thereafter.

I go back into the kitchen to get water for the birds. Pen's busily reading a cookbook.

"What's up?" I ask, but she just smiles and goes back to reading.

I take the water back outside and then jump again as a pigeon flies into the coop while I'm standing there. It rings the bell and looks at me expectantly. I reach in, pull the message from its leg, then, as an afterthought, give it some seed.

To: Miss Aurora Foyle

I trust you slept well. Put the pigeons to good use. They're on loan indefinitely. They're not for eating.

I look forward to dinner.

Caligula Green
Zombie Hunter Extraordinaire

I grab a pigeon that looks like it needs a workout and quickly write a note, then roll it up and stuff it into the holder on its leg.

To: Caligula Green

Read the contract then had weird dreams. You are one sick fuck. Of course, we won't

eat the pigeons. Down here in the slums we
prefer rats.

Best regards,

Aurora Foyle

P.S.: What are you wearing?

I draw a realistic heart, one that looks like it's been
ripped out of a fresh corpse, right above my signature. *My
handwriting is perfect, much better than his,* I note. My inner
schoolmarm high-fives my competitive streak.

Then I release the bird into the air. It flies up and
away. Seconds after it's out of sight, another pigeon arrives
and rings the bell.

To: Miss Aurora Foyle

Get your questions ready. But hold them
until dinner tonight. I've got to go kill a few
of the undead to work up an appetite.

Laters,

Caligula Green
Zombie Hunter Extraordinaire

P.S.: I've eaten my share of rats, too.

My heart races as I read his note. *A date! For tonight!* I send another pigeon off immediately.

To: Caligula Green

What are you doing? I'm bored.

Aurora Foyle

This time, the reply takes a little longer to arrive. The handwriting is shaky and it's spattered with what looks like blood and bile. *Is that a bite mark on the paper?*

To: Aurora

A little busy. Please stop distracting me and review section 13.18 of the Service Provisions of the contract. See you tonight.

Caligula

I read his note and sigh. Then I grab another small slip of paper.

To: Caligula Green

But I miss you.

Aurora Foyle

The pigeon that arrives a few minutes later looks more wide-eyed than the others. It's missing some feathers.

A:

Quit fucking around with these pigeons. A zombie almost ate this one. Do you know how hard it is to train these things to find me? Especially when I'm out in the field?

-C

No skull this time. Just a bloody fingerprint. I hope it isn't Caligula's.

I pat the pigeons on their bobbing little heads and tell them to rest for awhile.

"Well, that was interesting," I say to Pen once I'm back in the apartment. She's now sharpening a knife in the kitchen, whistling.

"Uh huh," she says, distracted.

I smile to myself, wondering what I'll wear on my date tonight. There is something so *hot* about instant communication!

CHAPTER TWELVE

Later, I get a strange urge to get out of the apartment so I throw on some old jeans and my leather boots. *Mr. Control Freak is already getting to me!* Before leaving, I send a quick note to Caligula, just to mess with his head. After all, his contract -- not to mention that freaky story about his mother's best friend -- certainly messed with mine.

I hug myself as I watch the pigeon fly off toward his tower downtown. He must be home today.

To: Caligula Green

It's been nice knowing you. And kinda gross. But very filling.

ttfn

Ro

Damn I'm funny! My inner schoolmarm looks at me over her glasses, which hang from a jeweled chain. I may be funny but apparently my grammar's not up to snuff.

I head out into the neighborhood, my gun stuffed into the back pocket of my jeans. I usually don't go out alone and know it's not exactly safe, but if I'm going to fight zombies, I have to be able to run.

I jog through the streets, taking in the abandoned cars and boarded up shops and the small groups of humans that are always hunkered in front of the old Starbucks. They ran out of coffee beans years ago, but people still gather there, brewing their own blend of tree bark and beetles and whatever else they think might work.

I jog past the people to an empty side street. There, I practice jumping up on the hoods of cars and zigzagging my way up the street around wrecks and wreckage. It's like my own personal obstacle course. Back in the day, women used to pay hundreds of dollars for retired drill sergeants to put them through these kinds of boot camp basics. All so they could fit into their wedding dresses or look hot for high school reunions. Today, it's about making it through the day, or maybe the end of the week, without getting bit by a cheerleader from your high school. Or your former groom.

Times certainly do change! Except when it comes to my out of control hair, that is.

I find another hair tie and secure my dazzlingly thick mop at the nape of my neck. *I can't believe he asked me to shave it off!* Then I continue to turn and dodge and jog my way through the dirty streets, thinking about his stupid contract the whole way.

Do I sign the thing and become number sixteen or seventeen or eighteen or, who knows, ninety-seventh in a long line of zombie killing assistants? Do I willingly become zombie bait? Or do I ignore Caligula and his strange yet wildly seductive and super hot proposition and carry on as before?

My inner sex goddess hooks an index finger in her mouth and pulls. *Be the bait! Be the bait!* she implores me with fishy eyes.

I'm not so sure that's the right answer, though. Sure, I might not last as long if I choose to fend for myself, but it's not like I've been completely helpless these last few years.

I bite my lip as I scan the streets looking for roamers and think back.

Actually you've been pretty lame at this whole survival thing, my subconscious reminds me. *If it hadn't been for Pen and Hoser and Paul not to mention those three guys who died protecting you while you were foraging for hair products at that abandoned Gene Juarez Salon, you would have been dead long ago.*

Still, am I prepared to give him total control? I wonder. *Am I even capable of that?*

When I get back to the apartment, Caligula's standing in front of the door, quietly feeding the pigeons. He looks tired and more than a bit disheveled. The man needs a nap. He smells a bit like disinfectant so I know he's been hosed down after his zombie fight. I hope he's changed his clothes, too. I know he gets off on the smell of death but it's a total turn-off for me.

I get closer and get a whiff of Axe Body Spray. *Ugh, that's even worse.*

"Did you come over to clean the cage?" I ask, teasing him with my eyes.

"Your last pigeon warranted a personal reply," he explains. "May I?" He gestures to the door.

I nod and open the door to our apartment, silently counting the pigeons. *Weren't there six before?*

We go in and I lead him to my bedroom. Once we're inside I start to take his clothes off.

He stops me with a yawn. He's gesturing around at my vintage rock posters and my Beanie Baby collection. "I wondered what your room would look like."

"Ugh, you've been here before, Caligula," I remind him.

"Have I? I guess I'm more tired than I thought." He rubs his eyes.

My medulla oblongata wakes up. I think of embarrassing things -- slipping in the bathroom and winding up face-down in the toilet, the first time I ate an oyster, that time Pen and I...-- and I blush on purpose. When Caligula doesn't notice, I bite my lip.

"I'm not sure I'm capable," he says, "but I must make you stop biting that lip."

He pulls a ball gag out of his coat pocket.

"But I want to talk to you."

"I know. That makes one of us." He seems to come to life a bit as he straps it on my head, so I let him.

When I try to talk around it, the only sound I can make is strangely familiar, "Mrraggagakalalk!"

He seems to like the sound. He's out of his clothes before I can blink. He pushes me back onto the bed and pulls something else out of his coat pocket, which is now on the floor. It's a bag of ice. I could go for a cold drink. But he has other ideas.

"Your skin is so warm," he says. "I thought we'd cool it down to what I'm more accustomed to."

He puts the ice on my breast.

I imagine the ice will feel nice on my nipple. Teasing and tantalizing and oh so sensuous. But it's just cold. Freezing fucking cold. I'm about to push the ball gag aside and tell him to get the fuck off when he's suddenly between my legs and inside me.

"Is this nice?" he asks, as he thrusts away. "Is this the part of knowing me that you find most especially nice?"

He pounds harder, as if he's trying to break up concrete. I come instantly, even though I'm not really into it. It's just the way I'm built, I guess.

I assume he'll finish soon, too. But he doesn't. He keeps pounding away. The Hummel figurines mom gave me begin falling off their shelf and breaking on the floor. Pen begins to bang on the wall. Caligula keeps at it.

"Do you have a jackhammer in there?" she shouts from the next room.

"Murrrggghh!" I offer.

"Ah, a BJ, got it."

I go deliciously numb. *I didn't realize someone could literally fuck your brains out. I always thought it was an expression.*

Caligula finally shudders, squeaks, and falls to the bed beside me.

"That's better," he mumbles, taking a moment to rake his long fingers through his hair. He looks victorious and more sleepy than ever.

I take off the gag while he starts to snore gently.

I hop out of the bed and grab some long-sleeve shirts, surreptitiously tying his arms and legs to the bed frame. When he opens his mouth, snoring, I jam the ball gag in. He comes awake as I strap it to his head. He can't get free. Little wonder -- I did get an A in my knot tying class.

"I'm going to get a drink," I say, leaving the room.

I go out to the kitchen, crack open my last soda and pour it into a glass. Then I drop what's left of the ice into it.

Pen looks up at me from where she's sitting on the couch. She raises an eyebrow but I just shrug. I don't feel like breaking the moment with a bunch of chitchat. She pouts, disappointed, and I take my cola back into my bedroom and close the door.

"I want to touch you," I tell Caligula. He's wide-eyed. He looks freaked. "So I'm going to. Now you're going to do what I want."

I put on my favorite pair of flannel pajamas, covered with kitties and puppies and unicorns. *They're adorable!* Then I climb into the bed next to him. He struggles a little as I fold myself around him but I keep pressing against him until we are officially cuddling. He's tense and his breathing is shallow but I don't think he's going to hyperventilate. I smell soap and sweat and something else that I have a hard time placing. *Fear?*

I run my fingers all over his body and begin to place gentle kisses on his face, his ears, his mouth, his nipples. He begins to squirm.

"Marharalajfdfd," he says, struggling against the gag.

"Yes, I'm going to take it off," I say. "But only if you promise to kiss me like you mean it."

He nods quickly. I remove the ball gag.

He gives me a nice, lingering kiss with just the right amount of tongue.

"I'm supposed to be the boss," he says, when we finish.

"I haven't signed your contract yet," I counter.

"You disagree with its contents?"

"I have some issues, yes. You don't get to dress me. And you don't get to cut my hair or bleach my skin. And if

I have to wear white all the time, I get to accessorize with accent colors, especially up around my eyes."

"But other than that you're in favor of the agreement?"

"I'm not sure. What would Rue McClanahan think of our relationship?"

"Rue who?"

"Your *Golden Girl*."

"She's dead so she doesn't think anything. Is this a joke?" he asks earnestly.

"No. I just think that whole undead cougar thing is pretty gross."

I can't compete with an old lady if that's what you're into! my inner inferiority complex shrieks.

"Gross?"

"Yes, gross. Plus it makes me wonder about your other ex-girlfriends or partners or bait or whatever you called them. Were they all old ladies? "

"You're jealous."

I blush, despite my best efforts and start to untie him. I've had enough of this game.

"Are you sending me home?"

"Yes."

He quietly rubs his wrists. Then gives me a cold, guarded look. "I can't wait until I'm the boss of you," he says.

"Please put your pants on before you leave." I don't want Pen to see what he's packing *down there*. I couldn't take the competition from my roommate.

I walk him out.

He gives me another kiss outside, by the pigeons.

"Let's put off our dinner until after your graduation," he says. "I need sleep. I also need to learn to walk again." He limps off into the night.

Back inside, Pen looks at me. "Are you okay?"

I take a deep breath. "I'm fine."

"Well your hair is a fucking mess."

She helps me fix it. *Time for girl talk!*

"So it would appear that you've got Caligula Green wrapped around your finger," she says, running a brush through my troublesome tresses.

I read that phrase in a Clairol ad once and have been dying to use it. Even if it's just in my head.

"You think?"

"I'm sure. He didn't stop on the way to your room to fuck me even though I offered." She finishes brushing out my hair.

I hear a bell and realize I have a new message. I go out to the pigeon coop.

To: Aurora Foyle

I look forward to your notes on the contract.

Until then, try douching with cold water *down there*. It should help with the swelling.

Caligula Green
Zombie Master

I smirk. *The killer of the undead is giving me advice on my lady parts?* I quickly dash off a note.

To: Caligula Green

I have a lot of issues with the contract. But
most of them boil down to the fact that I
want you to treat me right and not like one
of your interchangeable albino assistants!

Aurora Foyle
Bait to Be

I watch the pigeon fly away until it's out of sight
then turn toward the house. Just as I'm shutting the front
door, the bell goes off again.

To: Aurora Foyle

Go to sleep. You're going to need your wits
about you at your graduation. And you're
going to need all your strength afterwards, I
promise.

Caligula Green
Zombie Hunting Master

What is that supposed to mean? I roll my eyes and
scribble one last note and send it off.

To: Caligula Green

GO TO BED. AND DON'T YOU DARE
DREAM OF THAT OLD WOMAN YOU
USED TO FUCK!

Ro

I smirk, secretly hoping he hates shouty capitals.
Then I give the pigeons a final handful of seed and head
for bed. Tomorrow is going to be a big day.

CHAPTER THIRTEEN

It's the day before graduation. The mailman brings our weekly delivery and there's a card from my mom, along with a few newsletters: *Splat! The Official Voice of the Pigeon Keeper's Association* (Caligula must have signed me up), *Zombie Hunter's Anonymous,* and what passes for Seattle's newspaper, *The End Times.*

My mom has addressed my card in glitter glue. She's also attached a candle to the outside of the envelope, using a piece of duct tape. The thing looks more like a red wax tampon than a candle. Or maybe a butt plug. I've been doing some research.

Won't Caligula be surprised the next time we meet? My inner sex goddess rubs her hands together and snickers.

I decide the candle will make a fun mystery gift for him and try tying it to a pigeon. Unfortunately, it's too heavy. Or else the bird doesn't want to take it anywhere. It looks a little indignant. When I untie the thing it joins the other pigeons in the back of the coop, their heads cocking one way and the other.

Are you mocking me? my inner animal whisperer whispers. I shrug and go into the house to read my mom's letter.

As usual, she makes no sense. She's sorry she can't make my high school graduation and hopes prom goes well and that my date is a gentleman. She reminds me to fill out my scholarship applications so we'll be able to afford college. She thinks I will be majoring in Home Ec. Her husband also sends his regrets and congratulations. He's away on a fishing trip and can't wait for baseball season to begin.

I put the letter down, shaking my head.

My mother lives in la-la land. I don't need the terse doctor's note that's enclosed to know she still hasn't come back to reality. The outbreak was too much for a lot of people but it was especially too much for mom.

First, her sweet little kindergarteners all tried to eat her when the virus swept through the school during nap time (she climbed the school's jungle gym to safety). And then her husband was eaten while attending a Mariners game. Of course, a lot of people died that day, including most of Seattle's players who thought the fans were rushing the field to celebrate one of their rare wins. Turned out it was a pack of hungry dead racing for a snack. My mom was at home watching the whole thing on live TV.

I sigh, rereading her note. She still worries that I won't meet a well-to-do gentleman. How can I tell her that the gentlemen of Seattle are all zombie chow now. Sure, I'd love to find a nice, sensitive, loving boyfriend, but if I want to survive, I have to find someone who's almost as cold-blooded as the zombies.

Someone like Caligula.

My mom signs off the same way every time. "Love you honey. Hope you meet someone soon!" There's a little heart by her name.

Yes, Mom. I have met someone. I just don't think you'd approve.

I smile, picturing the two of them meeting. My mother, a Southern belle trapped in Seattle, would probably mistake Caligula, all in white, for Colonel Sanders.

Poor Mom.

A pigeon rings the bell and I put down the letter and hurry outside.

To: Aurora Foyle

I've been thinking about our issues. This brief tutorial may clarify them for you. In other words, I am so the boss of you.

master [mãs 'tər] -- **noun** 1. The motherfucking boss. He who is in charge. The grand pooh-bah.
2. see definition 1.

Synonyms: authority figure, skipper, employer, Charles in Charge, the man, maestro
Antonyms: underling, apprentice, worker bee, bait.

Caligula Green
MASTER Zombie Hunter

My lips twitch as I read his note. *To be honest, both sets do.* I hurry inside and grab a pen. It doesn't work. I grab another pen. It doesn't work. Third time, I get lucky. I scribble a quick reply.

To: Caligula Green

bait [b$\bar{a}$t] noun 1. the lure, the thing that
makes the hunt possible, the important part,
that without which you couldn't do your
job

mastur-bate (m$\bar{a}$s'tər-b$\bar{a}$t') **verb** 1. to whack
off. See also: flog the bishop, walk the dog,
check the card catalog, say hello to your little friend. *Example:* Caligula Green did not
accede to Aurora Foyle's proposed contract
changes so she refused to fuck him and he
could only masturbate.

Regards,

Aurora Foyle

I quickly fasten the message to the pigeon's leg and
then throw it into the air. *I love our hot little exchanges and
can't wait for our date tonight!*

My inner body clock tells me I'm late for work so I
grab Velma and scoot off, wondering if this will be my last
day at the salvage store.

I hope so. When I get there it's crazy busy. Rumors
have been flying about a new load of supplies being
brought in from Ikea, and everyone and their brother is
there to see what they might be able to pick up. I fly
through the store, my hands full of orders. Flashlights,
welcome mats, Scandinavian particle board bookshelves:

everybody needs something, although what they're going to do with this crap is beyond me.

Just as I'm about to finish my shift, I spy greasy Paul leaning against a rack of toilet plungers, watching me. He's still wearing bandages.

"Want to change my dressings, baby?" he leers as I take off my apron and get ready to leave.

"Can't. I have to be somewhere."

"My face?"

I stop and stare him down. "No, but why don't you come along? I'm sure Caligula Green would love to see you again."

His eyes widen, and his mouth falls open. But it's not good enough. I pretend like I'm holding a baseball bat and hit one off into the rafters. He blanches and backs up, knocking over a box of screws which falls loudly onto the metal shelf below. I leave as every eye in the place turns to stare.

Outside the store, I realize that Caligula and I didn't discuss a meeting place. But that's nothing new. I pull a pigeon out of my purse and throw it in the air. Attached to its leg is a message letting him know where I'm headed.

When I arrive at the J & M Tavern in Pioneer Square, his bike is out front, guarded by an albino, of course.

I walk in, and all eyes are on me in an instant. But they're not looking at my ridiculously messy hair. They're looking to see if I'm shuffling slowly, and perhaps dragging some entrails behind me. For some reason, the J & M has always been popular with zombies. But then it seemed to cater to them even before the apocalypse.

As my eyes adjust to the darkness, I see a vision of white at the far corner of the bar. Caligula looks immacu-

late especially among the pockmarked and lice-ridden
drunks around him, all of whom are keeping their distance. I look like I've been sorting machine parts all day.
He seems surprised as I sidle up beside him and peck him
on the cheek.

"You clean up well," I say, plopping down on the
barstool.

"You look stunning. Unclean, but stunning."

I think he really means it.

"Would you like a drink?" he asks, his eyes twinkling.

"I'll take a double," I say.

He nods and pulls a bottle of pre-apocalypse vodka
from his coat pocket and pours some into a glass. He pours
chilled water from another bottle into a matching glass for
himself.

"No ice?" I tease.

He drops two cubes into my glass. I have no idea
where they come from. *His veins?* I don't ask any questions.

The vodka alone is worth a fortune. Vodka on ice?
It's like I'm drinking liquid gold.

I take a sip, aware that every eye in the place is on
us. But they know who he is and what he can do and no
one is going to mess with him.

Or with me! my inner badass adds.

I take a longer sip. "So how do you want to do
this?"

"I think it would be best to go through the contract
point by point in a death spiral of excruciating details," he
starts. "I'll note your objections, we'll discuss them at
length and then we'll come to an agreement that we can
both live with. So to speak, anyway."

He gives me a strained smile.

"After that, I'll have my people redraft the entire document. We'll go through it again one last time, discuss any additional concerns, typographical errors and/or dangling participles and then finally, we'll both sign."

I rouse myself from my stupor.

"That sounds soooooooo boring," I say. The vodka has gone to my head.

He stiffens. *And not in a -- oh never mind, you know that one already.*

"Perhaps," he says. "But it's thorough."

"How about we skip the hours of forced banter over this damned contract?" I tell him. "I'm not bleaching my hair. I'm not shaving my head. And you're not dressing me unless I really, really like the outfit. Also, I'm not doing anything that I don't want to do, and I can pretty much tell you right now, anal fisting a zombie is something I don't want to do. As for the rest of it, you're going to use me to catch zombies and then you're going to use me in the bedroom. And that works for me."

He blinks a few times. If I'm not mistaken, he's bewildered.

I take another sip of the vodka and give him a wide grin.

"Now feed me, get me a little drunker, then take me back to your place and fuck my brains out," I tell him. "As long as your mother isn't on the loose."

He looks a little stunned, and he's staring at my ear. I blush.

"'Fuck my brains out' is just an expression," I tell him quietly. "I don't literally want you to do that. Sorry."

He pours me another vodka, and I take another long pull. He sips at his water.

It dawns on me that he's probably gone through this charade a dozen or more times with his other assistants. None of whom are still alive. *How long will I last with this madman?*

"Let's go to my place," he says, huskily.

It's too late. I'm mercurial as mercury.

"No way. I'm not in the mood anymore," I answer. "Sorry, you shouldn't have given me time to consider everything. Now I'm going home." I try to stand. My legs are wobbling.

"You're driving me insane, Aurora," he says, catching me.

"The bait isn't supposed to be easy to catch," I tell him, shoving him away. I take a moment to get my balance, then stagger out of the bar.

Outside, the albino is holding my scooter.

"Velma! My trusty steed!" I shout, high-fiving the albino.

Caligula's right behind me. He's not happy.

"You drive *that*?" he nearly shouts at me. "Moreover, you *named* that?"

I roll my eyes, flick my hair over my right shoulder, then cross my arms in front of me. Pen calls this the imperious princess pose.

"It gets me around," I say with a snort.

"I'll get you a better ride," he says. "Something that runs on gas."

"I wouldn't mind having a bike like yours," I blurt out before I can stop myself. "But I still won't let you fuck my ear."

He looks hurt.

"And you're really going home? I had my staff prepare some fresh cod."

"Let the cod cool," I say, haughtily turning my back on him. "You seem to like cold fish."

I can hear him sighing behind me. I pause.

"What do you want from me, Aurora?" he finally asks.

I slowly turn around. "I want to be part of your life. Not part of your afterlife." I bite my lip and look up at him through my tousled hair.

"I could *make* you stay," he says softly.

I chew my lip a bit. He chews my lip a bit. Then he gives me his jacket, which smells like marzipan. He drives me home on his bike.

* * *

I'm alone in my room with the lights out when I hear the tinkle of the pigeon bell. I immediately run outside to find a message waiting for me.

To: Aurora Foyle

You use sex as a weapon. I use my weapons as sex. Two can play at the game of hard to get. I hope you're satisfied and thinking. I hope you're considering the contract and that you're considering steering clear of me. I want to make our partnership work. But it has to be quick. I'm not used to the living in my life. I'm not used to making love. I'm only used to making death.

Caligula Green

I stare at the note, bewildered.

Geez, is this guy's first language even English?

If he's European or Russian or something that would at least explain the great hair and the monochromatic dress code.

I go back to my room and hug my pillow between my legs, trying to act like it's something more significant *down there.*

But it's just a piece of dirty foam.

CHAPTER FOURTEEN

Caligula Green is wearing a chewed up white T-shirt and little else. In one hand he holds a white riding crop, in the other he holds the reins. He's riding a zombie bareback like an old-timey cowboy, sans the ten-gallon hat. I'm naked and spread-eagled, tied to an old train track as a steam locomotive barrels toward me. I want him to save me. But then I realize that he's riding *me*, that the gag in my mouth is the bit in the zombie's mouth, and that, without the zombie, we've got nowhere to go. I want him to move! He kicks his spurs into my pink button and at the last instant flicks me on the ass with the lash. I barely get out of the way of the train. I can smell the leather of his jacket and feel the train going past, narrowly missing both of us. I can taste the metal of the bit in my mouth and my own fear. The rush of the fast, hot air on my skin and his spur in my clit make me come.

I wake up feeling like I've just been in a wonderful train wreck, my skin tingling all over. And immediately come again.

Pen looks me up and down when I finally stagger into the kitchen.

"Dinner must have been pretty good," she says wryly.

I'm wearing Caligula's jacket and a pair of underpants. I give her a wide smile.

"It was fabulous," I tell her. "I had some real vodka plus he hates Velma so much I'm probably going to get my own motorcycle."

Pen shrieks and keeps shrieking until I promise to give her a ride.

I wish I could be that excited. I don't know if I have the stomach to be his bait even if I love the sex afterwards. *Is his arousal going to help keep me safe? Or will it distract him at the wrong moment? And what about when he's done with me, will we part as friends or will he simply throw me over the wall to be eaten?*

Talk about bad breakups.

I absently eat dry granola as I think about my predicament. I've always thought of myself as a wimp but I've definitely gotten stronger in the last few days. I've killed two zombies with my bare hands. Well, okay I had gloves on. And I know I can kill more. Many more.

But I'm terrified of getting bit. Of coming down with the virus. Of dying, then coming back from the dead only to lurch through the streets like a gray-green scarecrow, trying to bite my neighbors and friends. Trying to bite Caligula.

My inner sex goddess ties a bib around her neck and sits down at a table, knife and fork in hand. She's ready to tuck into him right now.

But wait -- I might get a motorcycle!

Everything fades into the background as I fantasize about my cool new black bike. Then that fades as I realize I need to get ready for graduation!

Pen and I quickly get dressed in our Survival School caps and gowns. Neither of us has family attending -- they're all dead or zombified or, like my mom, too out of it to join in the fun -- but we know our classmates, teachers, and friends will be there.

Well, the friends that are still alive. I start thinking about Hoser. And the students who died during training, back when they first had us try to take on real zombies. It seems like most of the ones who died were teamed up with me.

"All ready?" Pen asks at the front door, and I nod. I open the door and gasp. The entire doorway is filled with another albino. He's gigantic.

How many of these guys does he have?

"Mr. Green knew you'd both be alone," the albino says. "So he sent me to escort you."

He offers each of us an arm and leads us down the recently swept path from our Pioneer Square apartment to campus. Pen immediately starts flirting with the guy, making me wonder if he was the one who provided her with the "entertainment" a few days ago. I even start to admire his bulging muscles as we walk toward the school. He's no Caligula Green but some of these albinos are starting to grow on me.

Survival School used to be a Japanese grocery store called Uwajimaya. Back in the day, people used to come here to shop or just stare at the crazy fruits and vegetables and grotesque animal parts. Now it's divided into a series of spaces used for instruction. Our teachers live in the apartments overhead.

As with a lot of the buildings in the city, the roofs are cultivated; ditto for what used to be the parking lot. The fruits and vegetables are a lot more boring these days, but they're edible, which is what counts, I suppose.

Would it kill them to plant a couple of star fruit or an acai tree? my inner elitist whines.

The graduation ceremony is in the old food court, where a bunch of folding chairs have been set up. None of the restaurants are there any more; just the signs. I stare at one advertising bubble tea. It used to make me hungry. Now the thought of black tapioca balls floating in a taro shake just reminds me of the stuff that came out of the zombie's throat the other night.

The albino stops at the last row of chairs, and we thank him, then go forward and take our place with the other sixteen students. We're right up front. Friends and a handful of family members are sitting directly behind us.

Caligula comes in and walks up to the stage and my heart immediately starts fluttering. I knew he would be here but it's not often that I've seen him with other people around. Other than his ghostly staff, anyway.

He takes his seat on the dais at the front of the room next to the teachers and faculty and a few members of the ruling council. He glows under the lights. *Or maybe that's just me.* Everyone else is in black. He's wearing his reflective rain gear, complete with axe and shotgun, ready for action.

He stares at me, and I blush. He leans toward me and stares more intensely.

I bite my lip. I want to see him get hard, to know he wants me. But then the chancellor gets up and drones on for a bit. He not only blocks my view of Caligula -- and his pants -- he tries to put everyone to sleep with assorted thank yous and salutations and had it not been for the generosity ofs. Staying awake through his interminable speech has by far been the most difficult aspect of Survival School. It's even worse than Rendering 101.

"That dude is so hot!" one of my classmates whispers as he nods toward Caligula.

"He's not gay," I whisper back. "And he's mine. Fuck off."

I can tell he doesn't believe me. He gives me the once-over, then looks up at Caligula. Then looks back at me. *I know it doesn't make sense. What would someone so rich, so powerful, so hot want with me? It doesn't add up.*

Yes, it does, my inner math teacher chimes in. *One is the loneliest number.*

"Jesus, what am I going to have to do to shut that guy up?" Pen whispers a little too loud. "Fuck him?"

The Chancellor stops mid-sentence, looks at Pen, and raises his eyebrows. For her sake, I hope sound doesn't carry. He wipes some dried spittle from the corner of his mouth onto his robe, then abruptly introduces Pen.

Pen looks out at the crowd, slowly adjusts her boobs and then starts.

"What's next after college? Survival! Duh!"

Everyone laughs and cheers, and I notice even Caligula is looking at her now. *What is he thinking? If she'd done the interview, would it be her with him now?*

At the end of her speech, Pen pantomimes adjusting her boobs again. *She's so funny!* Then everyone breaks into wild applause. I clap, too, although I've missed the whole thing, lost in my thoughts.

The Chancellor starts for the podium again but Caligula bounds from his seat and waves him off.

"It's okay, everyone knows who I am," he says. "And if they don't, they soon will."

At the podium he takes a breath and stares above our heads at the painted Survival School logo behind us. It's a bloody skull cracked in half with a rainbow behind it. I think he's probably confused because I don't get it, either.

I'm uneasy because he's not looking at me. Everyone turns to follow his gaze.

Then there's a loud *thunk* and our heads whip back around to face the podium.

Caligula has stuck his hatchet into the top of the podium. Now he's looking at us. And he doesn't look happy. Everyone's holding their breath, including me.

"I'm a major benefactor of this school," he says. "I helped found it. I helped mold you, create you, transform you into lean, mean, zombie fighting machines. I came here today to talk to you about the great things that are in store for you. About the great things in store for our city. I came to talk to you about how you would help me with my mission to figure out how to feed everyone and re-establish civilization. This is very personal for me."

There are a few scattered bits of applause. And a couple of wolf whistles. *Oops.*

"But I'm not going to talk about that today," he says, staring out at the crowd. His eyes are dark, swirling with anger. I'm glad he's not looking at me now.

"We're going to talk about something else. I hear some of you want to be farmers, that you want to grow food to help feed your friends and family and neighbors."

He slowly pulls his hatchet from the podium.

"Well, people aren't the only ones who are hungry," he says, his voice growing louder. "The dead are hungry, too. And Seattle is the buffet."

He pauses, his hatchet raised over his head. The crowd is completely silent, even the gay guy beside me seems to have lost his hard-on for Caligula.

"I *thought* you were being taught to kill," he says, pounding the head of his hatchet on the podium with each point. "That you would leave here masters in the art of zombie destruction. But then I discovered the school is a joke. It's Halloween High. Your teachers dress up like the dead to scare you kiddies and that's it! They're sending you out into the world completely unprepared. I found out that you had a *written* final." He spits out the word "written" as if it's poison in his mouth.

He takes a deep breath, looks up and nods. I see movement out of the corner of my eye and recognize Trafalgar. Or maybe it's one of the other ones. I look behind me. Ten albinos have suddenly appeared along the edges of the room. They weave chains through the exits and then padlock them together.

"Well, this is your final final." Caligula stares at us. "Miss Foyle, please join me on stage."

I gawk then stand up and shakily walk toward him. He offers me a hand so that I can make the big step up. The lights shine on me.

"Miss Foyle has agreed to join me in my zombie hunting work," he says. "She has flowered under my instruction, even though it has not been easy." He looks at me and gives me a sad smile, then turns back to the students.

"I'm not going easy on you, either."

I hear moans from the place that used to be a pho restaurant. It's our science and anatomy lab now.

"Let me show you how it's done." He claps his hands twice. "Trafalgar!"

The albino near the door to the lab opens it, and three zombies come racing out. They're fresh and fast and they make a beeline for the front of the room. There's a high scream. It's the chancellor. He doesn't realize the zombies are running straight for me.

"Mmaararrarrarr!" they harmonize.

Just as the closest one is reaching for me, Caligula becomes a blur. The hatchet chops off the thing's hand at the wrist. When it falls to the floor, it crawls away toward the girl next to Pen, who kicks it away like an oversized spider.

The first zombie keeps reaching for me with the hand that isn't there. Caligula kicks it in the face, and it topples backwards, into the second zombie. The two fall backwards onto the floor, one atop the other. The third trips over the two and does a face plant onto the edge of the stage. Teeth fly into the audience as Caligula stomps the back of its head to mush.

I let out a shaky breath, realizing that he's showing off, enjoying himself.

Things would be so much easier if he just played a sport, my inner soccer mom chides.

I look down and see that the first zombie is reaching for me again, this time with an actual hand.

"Caligula!" I scream as the thing claws at my foot.

He immediately steps behind it and spins it around by its neck. But it can't turn that far, and within seconds he's just holding a head. Meanwhile, the one on the floor has gotten back to its feet. Caligula hands it his hatchet, puts it right into a grasping hand. The thing looks at it quizzically for a moment then drops it and begins to bat at my robe instead.

Caligula steps between it and the audience and puts his shotgun to the zombie's head. He blows its brains out with an explosion that fills the room. I duck as gray and red goop rains down on me and the faculty members huddling behind the podium.

My math teacher starts to dry heave at the back of the stage. The chancellor looks pissed. But the students and teachers go crazy, cheering and applauding. Caligula takes the stage to a wild ovation.

"Please. Please. Sit down everyone," he says, breathing huskily. He rakes his fingers through his hair and grins out at the crowd. "So you liked that? Well then you're going to love this."

He pauses dramatically, then nods to Trafalgar again.

Uh oh.

Caligula grins, then suddenly shouts: "Everybody, look under your seats!"

There's a mad scramble as students immediately duck forward and start clawing at the bottom of their metal chairs. The gay guy I was sitting next to pulls out a tire iron, duct tape flapping from it like tiny wings. Pen waves a handgun at me wildly. I pray the thing's not loaded.

"Hurry up, everyone!" Caligula calls from the stage. "Because I've got one more surprise in store for you."

"Do you think it's a field trip?" I hear someone ask. "Maybe we're going to Australia!"

"Everybody ready?" Caligula asks the crowd. "Let's see what you've got!"

He claps his hands twice and Trafalgar -- or whomever -- opens the door again. This time a dozen zombies come pouring into the room. I stand up, furiously looking around for a weapon.

Just as before, the zombies all start to lurch my way, but no one notices but me and Caligula.

The room is chaos. Students are off their chairs, wielding hatchets and hoes and hedge trimmers liked crazed gardeners. I see a grandmother sitting in a chair sobbing hysterically. I hear someone else laughing and

then their laughter dissolves into retching. Pen grabs a
metal chair and starts hitting zombies left and right like a
professional wrestler.

"Oh my god, it's my dad!" someone screams.

"I don't have my gun," I shout to Caligula. "Quick,
give me something!"

He shakes his head.

No?

"It's okay," he whispers. "I pulled their teeth."

Then he steps behind me, and I feel Pinocchio there
in his pants. *That wooden boy is all I can think about.*

A half hour later, the students have finished off the
zombies. They're disheveled and glassy-eyed and splat-
tered with gore, but a couple of them actually look satisfied. Not the two who were trampled to death in the me-
lee, of course. Some of the students start throwing glares at
me and Caligula and the faculty. I guess they're mad because none of us pitched in to help.

It's a cold world, bitches! my inner gangsta shouts at
them.

The chancellor is still shaking as he hands the di-
plomas to Caligula, who takes them and once again steps
up to the podium.

"Just step over the body parts and come up to the
stage as I call your name," he says to the crowd. He's positively cheerful now. I can still feel the glares from my
friends, though.

I guess they're jealous. Or perhaps angry that I'm
dating a psychopath. I have no idea, but I do know this
stunt hasn't helped my social or professional life. *How am I
supposed to go looking for work now?* He's basically peed on
me publicly, marking me as his territory. Now I'll *have* to
work for him. *What else can I do?*

I wonder if he pulled this stunt on purpose to isolate me even further. I look at Pen, who has the gun lodged between her breasts. She grins at me, and I know I still have her.

Soon, everyone, including me, has received a diploma, and we move into another part of the store to toast our accomplishment and allow the albinos to clean up the mess.

Caligula sidles up to me, carrying two glasses of what looks like champagne. For all I know it's battery acid.

"Thanks for making graduation so ... memorable," I say, blushing.

"You're more than welcome," he says. "I know you must think I'm harsh. But it had to be done. They had to receive at least a modicum of training."

I nod. He's right, of course. Even though his training killed my social life, along with the zombies.

"I've been thinking about your offer," I start.

"Yes?" he says. I suddenly have his undivided attention.

"Yes." I swallow hard. "I want more, Caligula."

"More?" he asks, his eyes puzzled.

I nod and swallow again. I try it again with some champagne. Even better.

"More," he whispers softly to himself, as if he's tasting the word for the very first time. "You know I won't bring you flowers or sing you love songs," he says, with a gentle smile.

I smile back.

"Fuck the flowers," I say. "I want that motorcycle you mentioned. And another gun, something larger, like a shotgun maybe. And lots of ammunition. Also I want my own albino. Maybe two."

I stop and take another sip. And swallow.

"You do all that, and I'm in," I say. "I'll be your bait. Oh wait. I forgot. You're going to be my boyfriend, too. Now I'm outta here."

I turn, find Pen, and the two of us head home for a couple shots of rotgut. It's been a day.

When we get there, there's a pigeon waiting for me. It's got a message from Caligula, of course, letting me know how hot I looked. And telling me he's on his way over.

I have a couple of shots with Pen, then go into my room and change out of my graduation clothes. I slip the gun he gave me into my back pocket.

From now on I have to be ready for anything.

CHAPTER FIFTEEN

I'm waiting for him when he arrives on his bike.

"Hi," I say, letting him in.

"Hi yourself," he says, then gives me a wide smile. He opens his coat, and I see a bottle of real vodka poking out from an inner pocket. "I thought we could celebrate your graduation. And the fact that you're going to become ... my assistant."

"You need to promise to keep me safe," I say, all seriousness.

He nods; the grin is gone.

"It's guaranteed, now that you've agreed to work with me."

"And you're going to be there for me in that other way, too?" Suddenly, I feel self-conscious, or maybe it's just the rotgut. I flush scarlet.

"I'll do my best." He doesn't seem that enthusiastic.

I want him to want me. To want to please me. To want me to want to please him. To want me to please him while he's wanting to please me. I want it all. I also want to quit thinking about all of this because it's very confusing.

I look up at Caligula and bite my lip.

"Don't over-think things," he says, as if peering into my very soul. "I'm going to bury you in things. You'll have every thing you want."

"I don't come cheap," I say.

"No, but you do come easily."

Is that a twinkle in his eye?

"Shall we go through the contract again?" he asks. "We still need to finish going though the soft limits."

He lays a stack of papers on our dining room table and starts to take his coat off.

"What are you, the last lawyer left in Seattle?" I scream at him, tossing the papers onto the ground. "That's all you talk about. Contract contract contract. I'm not going over that thing again. It bores me to tears. Plus it's not legally binding, anyway. Write whatever you want, and I'll sign. Just remember, if you piss me off, you'll regret it."

He stares at me, his face unreadable, then slowly shakes his head. Apparently, he really wanted to go through the whole thing again. Maybe it gets him off. I hope not.

He stoops and starts picking up papers. Once he's done, he jogs them against the table, then carefully folds the sheaf and puts it into his inside coat pocket.

"Come outside and see what I brought for you," he says.

"For me?" I ask, wide-eyed. *Why on earth would he bring anything for little old me?* my Southern belle oozes.

Parked outside the apartment is a red motorcycle. Blood red. Four albinos -- three men and a woman -- are gathered around it. One's polishing the gas tank. He steps back and gestures to it as if he's a spokesmodel.

And the price is right. The bike is totally hot. "Ssssssweeeeeeet!" I shout and hop onto Caligula, hugging him with both my hands and my legs. Oddly enough, I feel him immediately responding to me *down there.*

Is there a newly dead zombie around somewhere?

"I'm glad you like it," he says. "My people here will pack your stuff up and bring it back to the tower."

"Whatever," I say, one hand unbuttoning his shirt. I slip the other hand inside and head south. Caligula moans, and I begin to nibble on his neck. He groans and I nibble harder.

The man brought me a motorcycle! And it's not white! He gets me. He totally gets me!

"Your push scooter was too dangerous," he says, trying to maintain control. It's almost laughable, considering how his man thing continues to grow.

"Consider Velma retired," I whisper in his ear, then give his whatchamacallit a squeeze. "Although right now, I'd much rather ride this."

I hop off and drag him into our dining room, then spread him out on the table and tug down his pants. Mine are off in an instant and I'm on him before he can say a word.

I push him into me and gasp, my hands lost in his wonderful unruly auburn hair.

"Aurora, stop. This isn't the--"

I clench harder and he gives off a low moan. I start to buck and moan myself.

"You're bending my dick in half," he groans.

I stop bucking and tuck him back in. He's buried in me all the way. I grip his hair, then let my hands wander to his chest, his nipples, his lips.

"Feel all of me," he begs.

I do. And it's awesome. I love my bike. I come thinking about it, and he comes with me.

Only then do I notice that the albinos are carrying boxes out of my room. They hardly seem to notice us, except for one who gives me a wink as he's walking out of the apartment.

CHAPTER SIXTEEN

Light slowly works its way into my head. I'm in the air, floating amongst the clouds, close to the sun. Everything smells great. I open my eyes to see the skyline of Seattle below me. I'm cocooned in a down-filled comforter on a wonderful mattress in my new room in Caligula's tower. And next to me is the master zombie hunter himself, face-down in a puddle of his own drool. He looks like a spent fire extinguisher.

My fire is out, at least for the moment. But running my fingers through his wildly unruly hair may just reignite it.

As I reach out, he rolls over and looks at me. His languid eyes beg for mercy.

"Don't touch my hair," he murmurs.

"Because it's not in the contract?"

"Because it takes me forever to get it like this. Why do you think I sleep on my face?"

When he gets up, his hair is a perfectly coiffed mess of untamed gloriousness. I can feel mine sticking up in all the wrong places, like I slept in an electrical field.

"You spend a little too much time worrying about your hair," I tell him. I blink. I blink again. I've got something in my eye.

"I had a rough introduction to the world of hair care products," he says. "I don't want to burden you with the story."

What the hell? I had to hack the head off a zombie with a pocket knife but hair care is too personal?

I rub furiously at the corner of my eye and finally get at the thing. It's a tiny feather. Pigeon?

I look up and find him staring at me quizzically. "Is there something wrong?" he asks.

"Nothing other than the fact that you look hotter than me," I say. "But you already know that."

"True," he answers. "You were talking a bit in your sleep. Were you dreaming?"

I flush, bite my lip and nod, looking up at him through my messy hair.

"We were in a grade school," I tell him, pulling the comforter tightly around me. "You'd forgotten your weapons. And you were killing undead kids with a spork you found in the cafeteria."

Caligula stops dressing and looks at me, his eyes dark and swirling. "You're not taking this seriously."

"I had a soup ladle," I say. "But I was wearing those see-through lunch lady gloves, and the ladle kept slipping out of my hand."

"You need to fight zombies coldly and logically, even in your sleep, Aurora," he says. "This isn't a romantic comedy."

"No, this was more like softcore porn," I say, my hand casually finding my secret lady spot under the down. "After we killed the kiddies you had me on the time-out desk in the corner. It was really hot."

He's not smiling. He finishes dressing, then pulls me out of bed and leads me to the kitchen. We eat a huge meal -- him fully clothed, me in my underwear -- then kit-out in the workroom. There's a matching set of hooded rain gear there for me. It's red and is the exact same shade as my motorcycle. There are boots, too, in my size; naturally, they're comfortable, thick-soled, and black. My gloves fit like gloves.

Caligula fills his parka's exterior pockets with shotgun shells. He straps his hatchet to his hip.

All I've got is my axe handle. I've left my gun in the bedroom.

"Any chance I get something a little sharper?" I ask.

"Not until I'm convinced you won't split my skull open when we're in a fight," he says.

In the elevator on the way down to the garage, he lets one. At least I think it was him because I *know* it wasn't me.

"What is it about elevators, huh?" I ask, my eyes twinkling.

He doesn't respond, even when I bite my lip.

In the basement, I head toward my shiny new red bike but he stops me with a shake of his head.

"No, leave it," he says. "You'll need to have lessons first, especially where we're going. I'll drive."

He pulls the shotgun out of the holster at his back and attaches it near his bike's fuel tank. I climb on behind him.

He turns the key and the bike roars to life between my legs. Ditto for my you know what.

Oh my!

We head out of the garage and wind our way through the city streets and south to Pioneer Square. We pass by the salvage store and the Survival School, then head east, past the designated areas where they burn the dead, past rows and rows of abandoned houses. Now and then we see people scuttling along the street or peering out of windows -- scavengers, most likely, or zombie hunters looking for nests. But the place is mainly a ghost town. Even though I grew up close to here, I haven't been to this part of Seattle since the virus hit.

Then I see the wall under I-90. It's a huge conglomeration of corrugated metal, chain link fencing, cars, and concrete blocks. There's a gate that leads through it. I start to get nervous.

"Hey, where are you taking me anyway?" I shout at him over the roar of the bike.

He doesn't answer. And he barely stops, just nods at the guards as they quickly scurry to unbolt and unblock the gate.

This nutjob is taking you beyond the wall, my subconscious screams. *Jump off the bike and run! Now!*

But I don't move. I can't move. Part of me is terrified. But another part of me wants to see what's out there. To experience that adrenaline rush of being close to danger again. Of being ... bait.

As the gate creaks open, Caligula guns the bike, and we pass through. I thought the other side of the wall would be teeming with zombies trying to break through, but it's empty and quiet, as if the sky and wrecked cars and the mountains off in the distance are holding their breath, waiting for something.

Oh wait. I'm the one holding my breath. Duh.

I take a few gulps of air and suddenly things seem more normal. Well, except for the fact we're on the other side of the wall.

It is different here, though. The roads are more cluttered: no scavenging crews to push cars out of the way and drag off the dead. Plus, it's way overgrown.

Caligula climbs a hill along a residential street, although half the time we're up on sidewalks and driving through what used to be people's lawns. Now they look like hay fields.

Morning glory, moss and mold cover the front of the houses, the windows too, and the once pristine hedges that lined the driveways are now monstrous green walls, gnarled branches reaching to the sky like outstretched fingers.

The bike slows and takes a corner and then another and soon we stop in front of a low brick building. Despite the long grass and unpruned trees out front, my old elementary school looks amazingly normal. The play area -- all sand and colorful plastic equipment -- hasn't even been overrun by weeds or grass or dog-sized rabbits. The memory of running feet seems to be enough to keep anything from taking root.

He shuts off the bike, and there's absolute stillness around us.

I slowly take off my helmet. My eyes are wide.

"Scared?" He laughs. "Good. That's a perfect way to start."

I put the helmet on the seat, then grip my axe handle tightly at both ends.

"Hold it like a bat," he says. "Try to get a feel for your striking distance and make sure you stretch your arms out fully. Hit them when they're still far away. But don't swing too hard; you'll lose control. And don't miss. If you miss, you'll have to fight them up *close*."

He re-holsters his shotgun and walks slowly toward the front doors of the school.

"You know I went here when I was a kid," I say.

He slows his pace a tad but doesn't look at me.

"Of course," he says, after a moment. "Why else would I bring you here?"

He's walking carefully, paying attention to every sound. His head is pivoting left and right, and he's looking into every window. If there are any undead here, they would have heard the bike. And I know that if any of them come for us, I'm here to distract them, not to distract Caligula.

My life depends on me playing my role.

I grip my axe handle harder, wishing I'd brought my gun.

We reach the front of the school, and Caligula slowly opens a metal door. Inside the foyer, there are yellowed papers scattered everywhere. Some of them are streaked with blood and ink like someone died defending a mimeograph machine. Nothing moves except us.

Inside the front office, the dried remains of the school secretary sit at a desk. There's a protractor buried in her -- its -- skull.

I guess somebody else didn't like geometry, my inner class clown interjects.

"Is the principal's office as you remember it?" Caligula asks me after we step through the broken glass to the inner office.

"Uh, not quite," I say, trying to avoid looking at the carnage on the floor. *Is that a rib cage? A bird cage? A model of the Space Needle?* "The last time I was here there was only one dead body. And Mr. Matheson's diploma was on the wall, not the floor."

Caligula roots around on top of the desk, then starts opening drawers. He comes out with the principal's paddle. There are thumb-sized holes drilled through the inch-thick wood at regular intervals.

"Does this bring back any bad memories?" he asks, smelling the paddle.

I stare at him, trying to figure out if he's being serious or if he's the sickest practical joker in the universe.

Did he bring me here for fun?

"Why?" I ask. "Are you going to spank me?"

That's when I hear it. The shuffling. Out in the hall.

"No," he says, serious. "I'm going to train you. Follow me. Quickly."

He leaves the principal's office and opens the outer door a crack so we can peer into the hallway. I see a crowd of shapes slowly shuffling away from us toward the classrooms. There are a few zombie kids but most of them are adults. I see men in suits, coveralls; a woman wearing scrubs.

"This place must have turned during a PTSA meeting," he whispers over his shoulder. "Hurry."

We duck out of the doorway and head toward two metal doors just to the left of the office. The gym. Caligula pushes open a door and, once we're inside, shoves a flagpole through the handles to keep them closed.

"This won't hold them for long," he says. "Identify a safe haven."

"My room in your tower."

"Not an option, Aurora," he snaps. "Look around you."

The bleachers are unfolded with stacks of folding chairs off to the sides. No sanctuary there.

My eyes land on the basketball hoops at each end of the gym. The nets are missing. *Eaten?*

"A backboard might be safe," I say.

"How are you going to get up there? Can you jump that high?"

"I could stand on a chair and jump."

"You'll fall and break your ankle," he says dismissively.

I keep scanning the empty gym, trying to find a place to hide. Or a way to escape. The windows are too high and the other doors are too far away. Worse yet, the doors we just came through are now moving. I can hear moaning from the other side.

"Brsaaaaaaaignnnnns!"

"We don't have much time, Aurora."

"You're not helping!"

"Look around. What do I have to do, send you a pigeon?"

That's when I see what he's talking about. The rope. A thick knotted rope hangs from the rafters of the gym like a ladder to heaven. We used to climb it when I was a kid. If you could touch the top of the gym, you got an A. If you couldn't get off the floor, you got an F. I never got more than a C.

"I'm not very good at climbing," I tell him.

"Perhaps you were never properly motivated."

The doors shudder and strain again, and I yelp and scurry to the corner, grabbing the rope with both hands.

"Use those legs!" Caligula yells as I start to climb. "I know how strong they are. I've had them wrapped around my head."

I make it about five feet up -- all the way to the third knot, farther than I ever made it back in the day -- when I begin to feel a strange, yet familiar, sensation *down there*.

I pause for a moment, thinking back, then inch a little higher. The sensation gets stronger. Now I remember why I never got more than a C.

The rope got me off, even back then.

"Keep going, Aurora!"

The door behind him suddenly bursts open and the zombies rush in. Well, rush is an exaggeration. They stagger. But there are a lot of them, and they still have their teeth. Some of them are still wearing hairnets and blood-stained cafeteria whites. They look like they're ready for a hot lunch.

With a start, I realize my old gym teacher, Mr. Austin, is among them. He used to sleep in a van in the parking lot and wore a comb-over that swirled around the top of his head like a cinnamon roll. Now it's undone and there's a giant curl trailing down his back.

Somehow he looks better green. *Weird.*

"Climb, you sloth!" Caligula shouts up at me. He's just a few yards from the horde but they're ignoring him and coming straight for me.

"Who are you calling a sloth?" I hiss as I pull myself up a few more feet. My face is flushed from the exertion and the impending orgasm and my breathing is so ragged it could beg for quarters on the street corner. I've got nothing left.

I hang on to the rope for dear life, my feet precariously perched on a knot, my lady parts afire.

"Okay, that's far enough, you weakling," he calls to me. "Now pull up the rope before they grab it and climb up to get you!"

I snatch the rope away, just in time, and haul it up toward me. My hands are burning and so are my shoulders. It's almost as bad as that time I took Zumba.

I try not to whimper, but I'm scared. I'm hurting, and I don't want to die. Plus, the bastard keeps calling me names.

What the fuck?

I cling to the rope, trying not to think about the smile on Caligula's face as he watches the zombies gather below me like cats waiting for cream.

A few reach up for me. Most can't touch me, but my gym teacher was more than just homeless. He was also super tall.

He starts batting the end of the rope with the tips of his fingers. When I try to pull it out of his reach, I slip and my butt drops. I feel a hand. It's Mr. Austin, slapping at my ass like it's a plump red tetherball.

"What the hell?" I shout at Caligula. "Are you going to get me out of this or are you just going to stand there grinning like an idiot?"

That's when I see him at the back of the crowd. He's taking them out quietly, one by one, but he's not using his gun or his axe. He's got the principal's paddle in his hands and is using it to bash their brains in.

He's not exactly taking his time, but he's luxuriating in the ease of it. I tighten my grip and try to inch my ass out of Mr. Austin's range. It's no use; my arms have nothing left. *I* have nothing left. The zombie keeps batting away at me like I'm a birthday piñata. It's demeaning and scary and, thanks to the rope rubbing against my lady parts, the teensiest bit hot. Apparently I'm becoming just as fucked up about sex as Caligula.

Just as I feel my grip slipping, he caves in Mr. Austin's head. The spanking stops and I drop the heavy rope to the gym floor.

"Well done, Aurora!" he says, tossing the paddle to the side. He wants to gloat; I want to split his skull with my axe handle.

I slowly climb down, stepping around the dead, as I try to stomp away from him.

"You're upset?" he says, his voice bewildered. He grabs my shoulder and spins me around. "What, did you want me to use the paddle on you, too?"

I roll a zombie's eyes at him with the toe of my boot, then head to my kindergarten classroom.

I know I have to rely on him to keep me safe, but I'm also tired of his weird drills. I almost got eaten, not to mention that I just had my ass spanked by a not-so-jolly green giant. Most upsetting of all -- I kind of liked it.

This whole zombie apocalypse thing is completely fucking with my head.

I want to go home. Or someplace that seems like home.

The classroom is empty when I push open the door. None of the windows are intact, but somehow the chairs are still on the desks, which are lined up in ragged rows.

The word "zombie" is written on the board in a teacher's careful block writing. I look around at a collection of pictures push-pinned to the walls. They're family pictures that the kids drew. Mommy. Daddy. Spot. I see a stick figure father eating a stick figure mother, head first.

I lower my head and start to cry. Suddenly, Caligula is at my side, his arm around my shoulder. He's stiff -- not his thingy, his demeanor -- but I can tell he's trying to offer something akin to comfort.

"I don't understand!" I wail into his shoulder. "Why did you do that? Why *would* you do that? I could have died! Or been infected!"

Unfortunately the only thing that comes out sounds like zombie-speak. "Ionunstahhhh. Whyduthaaaa? Whywuuuuuu? Icdddiiiiiiorbfffffft!"

Caligula pats the back of my head, gently.

"Shhhh, shhhhh," he says, comforting me.

"Thanks," I say, wiping my nose on his sleeve. My inner kindergartener saying hello, no doubt.

"I said shush," he snaps at me, his eyes on the door. There's shuffling in the hall. We wait until it passes, then leave the room and the hallway and go back out into the sunlight to the motorcycle.

"I know it's difficult, but it's important to confront potential issues," he says. "They make you vulnerable. This is how we'll do it, with easy training missions to known locations. You need to be able to handle the familiar in order to handle the unfamiliar."

I nod my head. It's not the strange zombies that you have to worry about. It's the people you used to know in places you used to know them.

Like Mr. Austin. Like Hoser.

I blink back tears and bite my lip so hard I taste blood.

He climbs on the bike, and I climb on behind him, silently gripping his waist as we wend our way back to the gate and finally home. There, we're stripped and cleaned by the albinos, who pay special attention to my hoohaw for some reason. Then I wave away Caligula's advances and head for my room.

I'm exhausted from all of the adrenaline. I'm also still not happy about the way things went this afternoon. *What has this man done to me? What am I becoming?* All I want to do is sleep. And dream of being a kid again.

Caligula sticks his head in just as I'm starting to drift off.

"Sleep well, Aurora," he says. "And stay safe, even in your dreams." He blows me a kiss.

My inner goddess isn't sure whether to give him the finger or blow him a kiss back. So she closes her eyes and dozes off instead.

You are completely fucked up, Caligula Green, I tell myself as I drift off to sleep on a soft bed piled high with impossibly soft, impossibly white pillows. *But you have a lot of awesome stuff.*

CHAPTER SEVENTEEN

I dream of one of my mother's sad candles and wake up crying.

Caligula is asleep next to me. Actually, he's on me, or at least half of him his. His leg is over mine, like he's a dog and was thinking about humping it, but he fell asleep before he could get motivated.

I think back to what happened in the school. *I could have died. I could have fucking died!* I try to move and realize I might die yet -- my body feels completely abused from climbing that stupid rope.

Hmmm. But there was that other part. I feel a delicious tingle in my nether regions and look over at Caligula. Yes, he put me in harm's way yesterday, but he also saved my ass.

Speaking of ass ... I slowly lift the covers to take a look at his.

"I love your inexperience," he says. He's been watching me, like a lizard. "It's exciting to see you scared. I don't feel that anymore."

"I never want to feel that again," I say.

"But don't you feel more alive this morning?" He stretches his beautiful muscles and smiles at me. His eyes are dreamy, and his hair is perfectly tousled. The guy's so hot he doesn't even have morning breath.

I can't believe I'm sharing a bed with this man!

"I'm just surprised I'm still here," I tell him, reaching for his man-thing.

He purses his lips.

"I think I've made you feel too safe," he says, ignoring me. "Which has led to you not taking things seriously enough."

His eyes get all dark and swirly, and he locks me with an intense stare. I let go of his man part and try my best to look like I'm paying attention.

Oh Jesus, not another lecture! my inner smart ass whines.

"We could both die out there, Aurora," he says. "And we *will* die if we don't focus. I wish I could tell you things will be easy, but they won't. We're going to be in a lot scarier situations than what you went through yesterday. But we'll get through them. We'll beat this plague into the ground and make the city safe again."

Oh my god! my inner psycho chick shrieks and immediately starts dancing around in my head. *He said "we!" He said "we!" He's talking about "us!"*

Caligula gets up and leaves my room, then immediately comes back with two balloons. One of them is a banana. The other is a Halloween zombie.

"I just wanted to congratulate you on your first mission outside the wall," he says, holding out the balloons. "You've made the choice to be here. And I know -- aside from the apartment and the motorcycle and the designer clothes and food and coffee and the albino servants -- I know it's been a difficult one."

I take the balloons from him.

"Thanks," I tell him, wondering if there's any chance I can get my hands on a real banana. And I'm not speaking euphemistically. I haven't had one since before the virus hit.

I sense he has more to say and look up at him through my tousled hair.

"I know this is hard for you, Aurora. You're quite willful. But you'll be much safer if you simply do what you're told," he tells me. For the four hundredth time. "And that means training. And eating. And never feeling bad about putting the dead down."

I nod and throw on some underwear, then the two of us eat a quick breakfast and get dressed. This time, it's workout gear. All in white, of course.

Doesn't this guy ever worry about pit stains? Sheesh.

Caligula leads me down the hallway toward the workshop but then opens a door opposite it. We're in a gym. Thankfully not one full of zombies.

He starts me out on the weight machines which I've never used before, but quickly master. I work my upper body, my chest, my core, my legs, then just as I'm about to collapse, he leads me to a pair of treadmills.

"Five miles," he tells me, climbing on one.

"Five miles?" I complain, then think about yesterday. Some day I might need to run five miles to get away from a shambling horde of zombies. I program the thing and begin running, first slowly and then after a while, as fast as I can. It's brutal but he's right there beside me, running even faster, sweating magnificently.

After we're thoroughly exhausted, he leads me over to a floor mat.

"I can barely stand," I protest.

"The dead aren't going to wait around until you're at 100 percent," he says, then starts to show me some moves.

I'm more interested in learning how to take off a partially decomposed head with a karate kick, but instead he shows me how to duck and dodge and break free of a hold. He plays zombie and soon, I'm sidestepping and shoving him around like a pro.

"Can you show me a few kicks? Or karate chops?" I ask, exhausted but eager to learn.

He shakes his head.

"Safety first," he says. "You can learn to tear them apart with your hands later. Let's try this a few more times."

I moan in protest and stagger around on the mats.

"Cute. You almost look like one of them. That could keep you safe for a bit, too, if you can keep it up under pressure."

Grateful for the break, I do another zombie imitation. Caligula stares a little more. I think of what I'd like to do to him and blush. Now he's even more interested.

I stagger over toward him.

"I could end your afterlife!" he says, getting into the role play.

"Mrrrrgggg," I offer. I keep moving toward him. Somehow my sweatpants have fallen to the floor. *Oops.*

He doesn't move so I take his head in my hands and fake chew the side of his neck.

"I could never hurt you, Aurora," he whispers into my shoulder. "If you turned, I don't know what I'd do."

I drag him to the ground and I chew a little harder. He whimpers like a baby. I continue to pretend to eat his neck, his chest, and his guts even as I'm riding him. I don't mind this final part of our workout.

We come together.

I leave him there on the floor where he's playing dead and stagger back to my room. After a quick shower there's a knock at my door.

It's Trafalgar. I think. He's got a stack of newsletters in his hands.

On top is *The Seattle Slut*, the most popular gossip rag in the city. On the first page is a grainy picture of the two of us labeled "Caligula Green and friend."

"Wow, I made the front page of the *Slut*!" I tell him, grinning.

Trafalgar looks at the picture, then looks at me. "He's a good man, you know," he says.

"He's also completely fucked up," I tell him.

He smiles and gives me a single nod. He's not so much agreeing as conceding the point.

"That's all I get, a nod?" I ask. "How about a little insight? Or some advice? I'd love to get out of here alive, you know."

The tall albino stares at me for a moment, then nods again and leaves.

Caligula comes in moments later. His eyes are excited.

"So you saw the *Slut*?" I ask, nodding at the newsletter on the bed.

"The slut?" he says, confused. "Well, yes, but that's no way to refer to her."

"Refer to who?" I ask.

It's whom, my inner grammarian pipes up.

"Refer to whom?" I correct myself.

"My mother," he says.

"Your mother? What does she have to do with any of this," I say.

"With any of -- Look, I just came in here to tell you that Mother wants you to join her and the rest of my family for dinner. Tonight. It's a celebration for your graduation. I've invited Pen, too."

Then he turns and leaves the room.

I stare after him. *The rest of the family? You mean there are more?*

I shake my head, wondering how I'm going to explain mombie to Pen, wondering what the hell the thing eats. I picture her grunting and Caligula asking me to please pass the brains.

I giggle and finish towel drying my hair. I suppose if things get too creepy, I can always put the serving spoon through her eye.

CHAPTER EIGHTEEN

The next couple of hours are about as exciting as a gynecological exam. I take an Epsom salt bath, catch up on some reading, stare out the window, practice blushing, then finally forage in the kitchen for some food.

I'm on the bed eating a salad when Caligula comes into my room to help me pick out an outfit for dinner.

"That salad was for tonight!" he says, his brow furrowing.

"It was in the fridge." I eat the last bite and make sure to crunch the crouton extra loudly.

He picks up the salad tongs from the serving bowl. He looks pissed. But when I blush, I can tell it's something else.

"Would you like to toss *my* salad?" I bat my eyes at him.

He grabs my legs and pulls them toward him, then pushes me down, right on top of my plate. I bite my lip and feel him pressing against my lady parts. Then I realize it's not him, it's the salad tongs. I start to protest.

"Quiet!" he breathes.

He starts pinching me with the tongs. First my lips, then my nipples, then he even picks at my secret lady button like it's the last piece of lettuce in the bowl.

After I come he starts to slather dressing all over his tremendous erection.

Did he work at a salad bar before the apocalypse? I'm curious, but don't want to ask. He's not finished yet.

He turns me over, and I manage to knock my plate off the bed. He thrusts himself into me and begins to bang me relentlessly. One might think this would get tiresome after awhile -- or that between the dressing and the pounding, I'd come down with some kind of urinary tract issue -- but instead it feels so impossibly good we both climax again within minutes.

"Hail Caesar!" he shouts as he comes. I glance up at him. He seems to be talking to the bottle of salad dressing he's holding.

At least he has one kink that doesn't involve the undead.

I use the sheet to wipe the dressing off my lady parts. Then crawl back under the covers and fall asleep.

CHAPTER NINETEEN

Caligula is chewing gently on my nose. "Aurora, get up."

"No."

He chews a little more insistently. I open my eyes. His teeth are yellow, rotten. I recoil.

"Gotcha!" he laughs. "These were my mother's!"

He pulls the teeth out of his mouth and slips them into his pocket. "I sometimes wear them to make her feel more comfortable," he tells me.

I shudder. *This guy is getting weirder by the day.*

"Could you not eat my face while I'm asleep," I grumble. "It's creepy."

"But we're late for dinner, Aurora," he says. "Come on, you need to get dressed."

Outside my window, the city is dark.

Fuck. I forgot about dinner with his "family." Even worse, I've been too busy training and getting tossed like a salad to warn Pen.

I hop into the shower to get the last vestiges of dressing off my skin. I towel my hair and put in some product. Still no dryer, but I'm lucky Caligula seems to like the wet look. Back in the bedroom, I find an outfit laid out for me on the bed, which is now made. As usual, there's a matching hair tie.

I don't know about Caligula, but I'm definitely starting to fall for the albinos.

I pick up the outfit -- a skin-tight white dress -- low-cut with capped sleeves and a pair of matching come-fuck-me heels. As usual, there's no bra or underpants. I throw on the dress and look in the mirror. My nipples and lady hairs are visible right through the material.

What's that about? Now that Mommy's a zombie he figures he can be a naughty boy?

Out of the corner of my eye, I see Caligula hovering in the hallway. He's dressed in an immaculately cut suit and tie. He comes into the room and kisses my shoulder.

"I want everyone to love you as much as I do," he says.

Wait. Did he just say that he loves me? I pause while my inner sex goddess and psycho chick do high-fiving back flips.

"Um ... shouldn't I have some protective clothing on?" I ask, pulling at the skimpy fabric.

"Not at all," he says. "It's a party."

Then he grabs me, and we're suddenly dancing to whatever music is playing in his head. When he dips me, his hands wander, and I'm happy enough to be without any underwear.

Oh my.

He continues to waltz me into the living room, his hands roaming over my body like a couple of zombies loose in the city. He lets me go as we enter, and I nonchalantly pull my dress down, exposing even more cleavage.

When I look up, I realize the "guests" have arrived.

There are four zombies in the room. Each has a thick metal collar around its neck and a large albino behind it. The albinos hold poles attached to the collars.

When I enter the room, they all seem to take notice of me. Then I see Pen. Her eyes are huge, but she's trying to hold it together. She also looks ultra hot in a little black dress that hugs her curves like no tomorrow. Which is probably good because there may be no tomorrow.

I walk over and give her a hug.

"Pen! I'm so happy you could come!"

"What? The? Fuck?" she whispers furiously.

I pretend she's talking about the dress. "Oh this? I know, it's pretty daring. Caligula picked it out."

I just can't face the truth right now. I'm living with an insane man and his undead relatives.

Grab her and run! my inner survivalist screams in my ear. *But leave the shoes. You won't make it past the elevator in those things!*

I step back from her, a blush creeping over my face. The zombies start pulling at their collars, trying to get closer to me.

"Msssrrghgggggggh!" one growls, tearing at its metal collar.

"Look," I tell Pen quietly. "Don't over-think things. Just eat as much of this excellent food as you can and then get the hell out of here."

Caligula leads two zombies over to us. One is his mother, dressed in her pearls and another Chanel suit. Her makeup has been freshened and she looks almost normal. Except for the fact that she has no teeth. And she's gnawing on her son's shoulder. The other is a tall, blonde man who looks a bit like Caligula. If Caligula were older. And greener.

"Aurora, you've already met my mother," he says. "This is my father, Carl."

Good zombie Carl.

His father is immaculately dressed in a light wool suit, his blonde hair as pale as the women in Caligula's reception area. Trafalgar is behind him, tightly holding onto the pole attached to his collar. Which is good since dear old dad apparently wants a taste of my face.

"Mraraggggghhh." Their moans form a two-part harmony.

"My father says you're very beautiful," Caligula says, smiling at me.

"Msssrrghgggggggh!" his mother chimes in.

"And Mother says it's lovely to see you again."

"Msssrsissshggggh!" Mombie says, shuffling closer and clawing at me with one hand. She's wearing gloves again. I look at the fingers to see if they're all there.

"What's that, Mother?" Caligula turns to the thing and listens attentively.

"Msssrpppsggggh! Msssghhhhuug!"

"Of course," he says, beaming at me again. "She says she'd like a hug."

I gulp and look over Mombie's shoulder at Trafalgar. Or at least, I think it's Trafalgar. He shrugs almost imperceptibly.

Does his shrug mean go ahead and do it? Does it mean, this is how he lost his last fifteen assistants? My inner neurotic goes through the possibilities one by one until I get sick of the whole scenario. I lean in and quickly give her a hug, then try to step back.

Unfortunately, she latches onto me as if I'm the last life preserver on the *Titanic*. Caligula has to pry her arms off me; I wince as I hear a soft snap.

"She's excited," he says. "I've never brought a girl home to dinner before."

"I can't imagine why not," Pen cracks, plucking another glass of wine from a serving tray. She downs it then reaches for another, giving me the stink-eye.

I look down and blush scarlet.

That's when the little girl tries to take a bite out of my leg. She's wearing a muzzle so I'm safe, but I can hear her teeth clicking behind the thing. Her albino handler gets control of her and pulls her away, just as Caligula goes down on one knee to introduce the two of us.

"This is my adopted little sister, Mina," he says. The zombie girl was Asian, apparently, but it's hard to tell because most of the skin on her face is missing, along with her lips. She's not even growling. She stares at me, her jaw working furiously behind the muzzle.

Click. Click click click. Click. Click click.

The last family member I meet is Caligula's brother, Eli. He's missing his nose and lower jaw, though thankfully the white hoodie he's wearing has been zipped all the way up to his one remaining lip.

"Ssososidnwwwqqqqgggh!" Eli bellows at me and Pen as we stare at him.

"Still trying to hit on the ladies, eh?" Caligula laughs and gives his brother a soft punch on the shoulder.

"Eli's always been a bit of a stud," he says. "He thinks the two of you are exceptionally hot."

Hit on by a zombie? This party just keeps getting weirder and weirder.

I look over at Pen; she's staring at Eli strangely. I raise my eyebrows at her.

"I think I fucked him once," she whispers.

Caligula ignores her as one of the albinos comes into the living room and rings a small gong.

"Dinner is ready," he says.

We shuffle and totter and drag ourselves to the formal dining room, which has a spectacular view of the city. The zombies sit across from us, their backs to the skyline. In front of us is a feast: roasted chicken (or pigeon?), grilled vegetables, salad, fresh bread and plenty of wine. *Thank god.*

Pen and I fill out plates. The zombies plates are already full of plastic food.

"Don't you just love the view?" I ask Pen.

"I'd love it more if it didn't include these corpses," she says around a mouthful of chicken.

"I'm so pleased you could join me and Aurora and the family for this little impromptu celebration," Caligula responds, ignoring her barb. "Mother wants to know where you got your dress, Aurora."

"It's just a little something your albinos whipped up out of tissue paper and spit," I tell him, smiling sweetly. "I feel practically naked in it."

He shifts in his seat. *Is he adjusting himself?*

"Yes, you look practically naked, too," he says. "Mother quite likes it."

I spit out a piece of carrot.

"Ask your mother how she keeps her skin looking so young and supple," Pen saying, laughing. Her plate is piled high with meat. She looks like she's eating for three. "It must be hard to look that good at -- what is she -- sixty-dead?"

"The secret is sunscreen. And staying out of the elements," Caligula offers. "That's my secret, too. Or one of them."

"If *this* is what's out in the open, I'd be worried about what else you might be hiding," Pen says through a bite of bread.

"Aurora knows everything," Caligula says calmly.

"Then Aurora had better have her head examined."

"Isn't the food great?" I ask, trying to keep the two of them from snapping at each other. I can't do anything about Mina snapping at me.

"Isn't your mother going to eat?" I ask Caligula.

"No, she eats like a bird," he says. "Well, she eats birds. She's already had a couple of starlings today."

Caligula's brother seems fixated on Pen. But his mom and dad and little sister only have eyes and appetites for me.

I take another bite of chicken and wash it down with a sip of wine. Then another, then another, and another.

"Don't overdo the wine, Aurora," Caligula chides me. "Remember your training."

Immediately, my face starts to heat up.

As I blush, Caligula's mom suddenly lets out a loud roar, and so does his dad. The brother follows, though it's more of a gurgle with his lower jaw missing. Caligula's sister's teeth clicking increases until it starts to sound like she's shivering.

Pen grins at me and roars back at the zombies, taunting them. They get louder. She gets louder. Soon, it's unbearable.

"You're upsetting them." Caligula yells at her over the racket.

"They're not upset," she yells at him. "They're dead. You're throwing a dinner party for the dead!"

"I invited you into my home!" he shouts at her.

"You invited me into a fucking charnel house!" she shouts back.

Caligula stands. He looks angry. Pen starts moaning -- it sounds more like a ghost or a banshee now -- and the zombies get more and more worked up. I watch Trafalgar's muscles bulging as he tries to keep Caligula's father in check.

I stand and put my hand on Caligula's arm.

"Give us a second, Pen," I say, taking Caligula's hand and heading toward the hall that leads to the workroom.

"You've got to stop antagonizing him," I whisper in her ear as we pass.

"He needs antagonizing. And you need a fucking reality check!" she hisses at my back.

Once Caligula and I are in the hallway, he glares at me, his eyes burning with anger. Or sunscreen. *I hate it when I get that stuff in my eye.*

"Your friend has atrocious manners," he spits.

"It's a lot to take in. And you probably didn't warn her about your family," I say. "I'd be freaking out, too."

In fact, I am freaking out. *But I know a quick way to reduce our stress.*

I raise my dress an inch and give a quiet moan, my best impersonation of his mother. Leaning closer, I begin to gnaw on his face.

"Mssjsjuwuwwghghgh?" I offer.

"Just keep your voice down," he growls. "I don't want my family to hear us."

CHAPTER TWENTY

Caligula bursts through the door to the workroom and claps the lights on. We're alone with the tools of our trade.

"That thing you were doing at the dining room table," he says, panting. "That thing with your legs. Do that some more."

What? I wasn't doing anything with my legs.

"Please, Aurora," he begs. "Do it some more."

Was Pen playing footsie with him under the table? Or worse, one of the zombies?

Ewww.

But I've got no time to puzzle this out. I just need to come and then get back to the table before Pen freaks out.

"No, I'm not going to do that thing with my legs," I tell him.

Caligula stops and stares at me.

"No one says no to me."

"No, no, no!" I shout at him.

His eyes go big, then narrow, then smolder, then swirl with anger, then look bemused, then finally close. When he opens them, he seems amused.

"Actually, that's pretty hot," he says. "Say that again."

"No," I tell him, planting his hands on my ass. He's interested now. I moan and chew at him for a few seconds, then I blush and bite my lip. Soon he's biting me back.

"You're mine," he whispers.

"I'm yours," I echo. *And it's probably true. After to-night, I'm not sure if even my best friend will have me.*

When he finally fucks me, it's quick and intense and it's only for him, but I come anyway. Three or four times.

We clean ourselves up quickly and are on our way back to the dining room, when we hear the commotion.

Coming around the corner, I see that one of the albinos, the one controlling Caligula's brother, isn't wearing any pants. He's got a weird, worried smirk on his face as he sees us. Pen is pulling her dress down.

"Two can play at the quickie game," she says and shrugs.

I blush. So does the albino.

Caligula's brother lunges at me, and the pole slips out of his handler's hands. Eli's quick because he's well-preserved, but I'm quicker and trip him. He falls onto a platter of chicken. The smell of meat seems to enrage him further, probably because of that whole missing jaw thing, and he spins around and lunges at me again. Mombie, dad and Mina begin to howl.

Cheering section?

Caligula pushes Eli down, then steps on the pole, pinning his brother to the ground.

"Such incompetence!" he shouts at the albino who's furiously trying to refasten his pants. "You're fired!"

The man goes pale again. Well, paler. The rest of the albinos exchange looks.

"I'm so sorry, Mr. Green," he says, rushing over. Unfortunately, Mina jumps at him, and he runs right through the pole attached to her neck, snapping it in half.

In a flash, the toothy little thing is making a beeline for Pen, who's staring out the window at the city, leisurely smoking a cigarette.

"Pen! Be careful!" I scream.

But Mina's already on her. Pen is shrieking. Eli's albino is blubbering at Caligula's feet, begging for forgiveness. Caligula can't move because if he does, his brother will be loose. Mombie and Dad are howling and straining against their keepers. And I can see the muzzle on Mina is starting to slip off.

In a second, she's going to be face-deep in my best friend. And not in a good way.

I race over and grab the broken stick at the back of Mina's neck, but I can't get a good grip. I put my fingers into her collar and feel my nails sinking into her flesh. I don't stop. I pull her off Pen.

Unfortunately, I pull her right on top of me. And I've knocked her muzzle completely off.

Click, click, click.

Staring up, I'm face to rotten face with Mina, who's snapping her baby teeth at me like they're castanets. She once had lips but they're long gone now. She probably chewed them off herself. She's certainly doing her best to chew mine off. *Must run in the family.*

I try to gouge out one of her eyes with my thumb but can't quite get at them. She's fast and keeps snapping at my digits. The best I can do is hold onto her neck and keep her off me.

"Aurora!" I hear Caligula shout.

Looking over, I see his mom gumming Pen's arm. My friend is freaked, but I know she's safe. Across the room, the fired albino is sitting on Caligula's brother, pinning him to the ground. Caligula's father is sitting at the dining room table moaning. He's holding a knife and fork in his hands -- properly. Apparently, not even death can fuck up good manners.

Click. Click, click. Mina is still snapping at me. *Funny time for my attention to wander but apparently my mind is doing one of those time-slowing-down things that they always include in action-adventure novels.*

Mina starts to struggle, and I realize Caligula has wrapped his arms around her neck and is pulling her off me.

"Go to the workroom!" he shouts. "Lock yourself in!"

"No! Save Pen!" I shout, standing up.

Caligula glances over at Pen, who's pushed up against the window as mombie gnaws on her neck.

"Those are just love bites," Caligula protests.

"Yes, but she doesn't know that!" I scream back. Pen is shrieking hysterically. Even though it sounds a bit like her fake screaming at the table earlier -- or her fake screaming while she's having really bad sex -- I can tell she means it. *Poor Pen. She thinks she's going to die!*

I run over and elbow Caligula's mother directly in the face. She staggers off to the side.

"You can't treat my mother like that!" Caligula shouts, letting go of his little sister in order to pick his mom up off the floor.

He looks up at me in horror. Our eyes lock and in one glance I see it all: his desire, his vulnerability, his fear, his revulsion, his strength, his exhaustion, his confusion and what looks like a little bit of gunk in the corner of his eye.

Unfortunately, I don't see his sister crawling toward him until it's too late.

"Aaaaaaggh!" Caligula roars and shakes his hand loose. Suddenly, the world stops. Mina grins up at us, her mouth full of meat and blood. Caligula huddles on the floor next to his mother, holding his hand. Pen begins screaming again but I think it's because Caligula sprayed blood on her dress.

I grab Mina by the collar with one hand and pick up a silver serving spoon with the other. Then I plunge it through her eye. She struggles for a moment then slumps and goes still.

I stomp a stiletto heel through the brother's eye socket next. The only soft limit there was his rotting skull. And then I walk up behind his father, who is trying to fork roast chicken into his mouth. Except he's using the wrong end of the fork. It takes me a few tries, but I'm finally able to twist his head off.

I save mombie for last. Caligula has her sitting in a chair now. She's cradling him while gently gnawing on his neck.

"Please, Aurora, please," Caligula protests. "She really does like you."

Too bad the feeling isn't mutual, my inner zombie hunter answers. I shove a pair of metal salad tongs up through her open mouth. They jut out of the top of her skull like little horns.

"What the fuck?" Pen shrieks between gasps. She's hyperventilating. The albinos are watching me as if awaiting orders.

"Get her on the couch and give her something to drink!" I shout at them, pointing at Pen. "And get Caligula to the workshop immediately!"

They scurry around, carrying out my commands.

Hmm, I could get used to this, my inner megalomaniac purrs.

I jog along beside Caligula as the albinos rush him down the hall to his workshop.

"I'm sorry I had to kill your family," I tell him.

"It's okay," he sobs. "I was adopted."

The albinos kick open the door and place him on the red leather couch in the middle of the room. I spy some used tissue from our earlier session on the floor and kick it under the couch. *Oopsie.*

Then I stare down at his hand. It's wrapped in a white dinner napkin although the thing's almost entirely crimson red with his blood at this point.

Caligula is moaning.

I put my hand on his forehead, stare deep into his eyes.

"Focus, Caligula, focus," I say, trying to sound as calm as I can. "Do you have enough of the antidote to give yourself?"

"Antidote?" he asks, confused.

Jesus, the virus is kicking in already!

"Yes, the serum. I know you've been working on a cure."

"What are you talking about?" he yells at me. "There's no cure. I'm completely fucked."

My mouth pops open.

"But what about all that stuff?" I point to all the chemistry equipment. The beakers. The test tubes. The Bunsen burners and convoluted habitrails of glass. "If you're not working on a cure, what *are* you working on?"

"It's a still," he says, wincing.

"A still? But it takes up a quarter of your workroom. I thought you were working on a cure."

"I was," he says. "A cure for bad booze. You seemed to like my vodka."

I walk over to one of the beakers and sniff at the clear liquid within. Then I shrug and take a shot.

CHAPTER TWENTY-ONE

I wake up the next morning with a hangover. Unfortunately, what I really want is a do-over.

It was bad enough living in a zombie apocalypse, but now my nutjob boyfriend's going to die -- and then come back -- in a few days. And my friend is probably not speaking to me because she almost got gummed to death by my formerly future former mother-in-law.

Also, you totally ruined that cool white dress, my inner perfectionist reminds me. *Could things get any fucking worse?*

I look down at Caligula, shivering in the bed beside me. All I wanted was to be safe. And maybe have some good sex on the side. And to live here in this tower with all of his cool stuff and a bunch of muscular albinos waiting on me hand and foot. All I wanted was to forget about how fucked the world had become.

Was that too much to ask?

Caligula opens his eyes. Maybe it's the harsh morning light or maybe it's the virus, but for the first time ever he looks ... average.

"Morning," I venture. I push his hair back from his face.

"Morning," he says. He doesn't even bother to admonish me about touching him. His voice is subdued. His man thing even more so.

"How are you feeling?" I ask.

"Hungry," he says, then smiles. "But not for brains. Not yet, anyway. Would you like some breakfast?"

As we leave my bedroom, one of the albinos comes in with fresh sheets. I give him a big smile. He smiles back then raises his eyebrows -- or what would be his eyebrows -- nodding toward Caligula.

I shrug.

Caligula is still walking tall and strong, but I can tell he's faking it. I peer into the dining room and see that it's been completely cleaned up. You'd never know four zombies had been killed there the night before.

"I think it's a Pop Tart kind of day," Caligula tells me, rummaging in his cupboards. He's using his uninjured hand, the one that wasn't bitten.

An albino appears with a shiny chrome toaster, which he plugs in. *They're being extra-attentive now*, I realize. *They know the end is near.*

Caligula opens a cupboard above the refrigerator and reaches far back into it, coming out with what must be his secret stash. It's a sealed box of raspberry Pop Tarts. They look like they're twenty years old.

"My mommy used to feed these to me," he says. "My real mommy. She was young, and she died young, but she was the best. She let me eat anything I wanted."

I smile and nod and try not to freak out over the fact that he's suddenly talking like a five-year-old. Somehow it's even creepier than everything else that's gone before: the weird zombie sex, his old dead girlfriend, that damn rope-climbing incident.

We sit in silence as the Pop Tarts toast, then continue to sit as they cool down. *I don't need a burned mouth on top of everything else that's gone wrong.*

As we eat, I try not to look at the bandage covering the wound on Caligula's hand. *The wound that's going to kill him shortly.*

Finally, it's too much.

"So, how much time do you have left?" I ask. "Three days? Four days? Five?"

He ignores me, closing his eyes as he chews his delicious toaster pastry.

"Hoser had five days before he turned," I say. "Do you think you'll have that long? Are there any preparations you'd like to make? Anything I can help with?"

I put my hand on his shoulder and stare into his face, biting my lip with concern. I know he's a nutcase, but he's been good to me in his own way. He opens his eyes and stares at my lip.

"Yes, there are some things you can help me with," he says.

After breakfast, he leads me back to the workroom. I think he's going to tell me the room's secrets. To beg me to keep up the fight after he's gone. To bequeath the keys to the palace. I figure he's going to take it like a man.

Instead, he wants to take it from me.

He hands me a strap-on harness and a dildo, then opens a drawer and reveals a vat of lube big enough to drown a pigeon in. The dildo is thick and white (of course) and is made of some kind of pliable rubber.

I strap the thing on and stand in front of him, my lady cock jutting up and out. Despite his fever, Caligula is already hard.

"You look so strong, so powerful," he says, touching my face with his good hand. "I know I can trust you to do the right thing. When the time comes."

"Of course," I say. "It's in the contract." *Which I still haven't signed.*

He smiles and his hands start exploring my body.

"Tell me what you want," I whisper to him. "Tell me how I can help."

"I want you to take charge," he says. I'm not sure if he's talking about sex or something else but I nod and push his hand down so it brushes against the dildo.

"Like this?" I ask.

He nods, and his voice becomes a husky whisper.

"Yes, like that," he says. "Take me, Aurora. Take me every which way but loose."

I nod and take a deep breath. *Time for a little role reversal*, my inner dominatrix says, cracking her whip.

"Yes, I'm going to take you," I say, scooping out a handful of lube. "I'm going to take you, and you're going to like it."

He whimpers and begins stroking himself with his good hand.

I pull him down onto his knees and push the dildo against his mouth.

"Taste it," I tell him. "Show me how much you like it."

He takes a tentative nibble, then opens his mouth and takes the whole thing in. I watch, fascinated, wondering if this is the real Caligula or if it's something the fever's brought on.

"Okay, that's enough. You're scraping it on your teeth," I tell him, pulling him to his feet with one hand as I lube up the dildo with the other. I turn him around and drape him over the armrest of the red leather couch.

"I'm going to fuck you now," I tell him. "And it's probably going to hurt like hell."

It's the right thing to say. He moans hard. A little too hard. He's starting to sound just like his mother.

I try not to think about that as I slowly push into him. I don't really want to hurt him but I can tell he needs distracting from that whole turning into a zombie thing. As he moans with pleasure, I look around at the work-shop. The weapons, the protective gear, the weird moving specimens, even the still.

What's going to happen to it all?

I think about the possibilities as I peg him. Some-one has to take charge, has to keep the city safe, and there's really no one else to do it except me. Would it be possible to continue to run the zombie hunts, the salvag-ing missions without anyone knowing Caligula was gone?

I'm suddenly seized with a rush of power. *So this is how it feels to be a master of the universe.* I start using my shiny white cock as a battering ram, the same way Calig-ula's done with me all those times. Before long, we're both coming like crazy. Simultaneously, of course.

Is there any other way to do it?

When I'm done, he's weeping, as is the wound on his hand. I pull out, unstrap, tousle his hair a little bit and then slap him on the ass.

"Did you like that, baby?" I ask.

He looks away, nodding. "Yes," he says quietly.

"Yes, what?" I ask.

"Yes, sir," he answers.

"Play your cards right, and there will be more where that came from," I tell him, then wander back to my room, passing a trio of albinos heading his way with hot, scented towels.

Back in my room, I dive onto the bed and immedi-ately break into sobs. I'm sick to death of zombies and undead viruses and people who are completely fucked up in the head because of them. All I want is to get away, to escape, to find something familiar before it's too late. Before I become as tainted as him.

After a while an idea occurs to me, and I quickly get up and throw on my motorcycle gear. I'm almost to the elevator when he catches up to me.

"Where are you going?" He looks even more disheveled than he did when I left him. I touch his forehead, and it's burning up. He's starting to give off a strange smell, too.

He's going fast.

"I'm going to my mother's," I say, comforted by the weight of the gun in my pocket. "I need to see her."

Also, you're sort of nuts and on the verge of turning into a zombie, my subconscious roars. *I need to get the fuck out of here!*

"I was hoping we'd get in a few more 'training sessions' before lunch," he says quietly.

"I'm not going to be fucking you when you turn, Caligula," I tell him.

He looks up at me, wounded.

"I'd never do that to you, Aurora. Besides, I've got some time."

"How much time?" I ask.

He shrugs. "Three days. Maybe four. I'd love to spend that time with you. I'd also love to meet your mother."

"My mother's not in a position to meet anyone," I tell him. "I don't even know if she'll recognize me. It's been a long time since I've seen her."

"Then I definitely need to come with you," he says. "For all you know, she could be undead. Stay here while I get my things."

He turns around and heads to his room and I sigh, waiting. The guy still wants to protect me, even though he'll soon be trying to tear out my throat. I suddenly feel like I'm dating a needy vampire.

We go downstairs and mount our respective bikes. Dressed in his leather, with his helmet protecting his face, it's impossible to tell there's anything wrong. Same hot body, same tight ass. The only indication that anything's changed is the fact he doesn't hassle me about taking my own ride.

Too tired to even boss me around. That can't be good.

I shake off the feeling of impending doom and try to enjoy the ride. It's a bright sunny day and the city seems alive, despite the fact that we're living in a world of death and decay. I follow Caligula as he wends his way through the city, narrowly missing abandoned cars and bicyclists and the other oddball traffic that fills the street. We pass skateboarders and people on push scooters and a few tired souls trudging uphill with shopping carts full of food, fleece vests, and other salvage. At one point he guns his bike to give a jaywalker a scare. I can almost see him grinning.

He's such a scamp! If only he weren't going to be dead soon! my inner psycho chick sighs.

After awhile, we go up and over Queen Anne Hill and down the backside, then he abruptly turns to the left and shuts off his bike. Naturally, he knows exactly where my mother lives, in a care center for the addled but useful. The guy's albino network must extend all over the city.

When we walk in, I see her immediately, hunched over at a tiny table doing finger painting. A caregiver is close by, ignoring her and everyone else in the room, her nose buried in a romance novel. Looking around, I see a doll house, some toy trains, a crib, and a fake kitchen set, complete with fake food. A forty-something woman is at the tiny stove, "heating up" a pan of what looks like fake spaghetti. I think of dinner last night and have to look away for a moment.

"Aurora! What a pleasant surprise!" My mom jumps up and greets me like I'm visiting her mansion in the deep South. She forgets the paint on her fingers and smears my coat with green and blue when she gives me a big hug.

"Child, you are a sight for sore eyes!" she says, pushing away and grabbing my arms. Now my sleeves are covered with paint, too.

Suddenly, she realizes I'm not alone and her eyes widen as she takes in Caligula. She gives him a wink, then turns to me.

"And who is this strapping young man you've brought with you?"

Strapping young man? I look over and see that Caligula is leaning against a wall, barely able to stand. His skin is at least thirty shades of gray, and he's rocking the worst case of helmet hair I've ever seen. It's obvious he doesn't have long.

"Mrs. Foyle, it's a delight to finally meet you," he says, kissing her hand. I reach for my gun, worried he might take a bite. Instead, he holds it gently between both of his and gives her a wide smile.

A cowlick boyishly flops down on his forehead, and he suddenly looks completely adorable again.

How does he do that? My inner stylist shakes her head in awe.

"Mrs. Foyle?" my mother simpers. "Oh please, call me Sandy." She turns to me and gives me a look. I can't tell if she's passing gas or wants to have sex with him. I pray it's not both, but the guy is just freaky enough that he might be into it.

"So what brings you to my humble abode?" she asks, clearing off her finger painting so we can join her at her tiny table.

As he sits, Caligula begins to cough. It gets wetter and louder and lasts for about three minutes, finally ending with a disturbingly dry rattle. I look over at him, worried he's taken his last breath, but he gives me and my mother a tight smile.

"Allergies," he says.

"Oh, I know just what you mean," Mother says as I sit down. "Everyone has them this time of year." She leans close and stage whispers to me, "This one's a keeper."

"Your mother is right," Caligula says to me. "I want you to keep me. You know. After."

"No. Fucking. Way," I tell him. "When you turn, that's the end. You're dead. I'm not going to turn you into one of those grease-painted ghouls you had back at the tower."

"My goodness, you two lovebirds have such intense energy," my mom offers. "I can practically feel the electricity from here!"

"Oh, sorry," Caligula says, reaching for his tool belt.

Damn cattle prod must be on the fritz again.

He looks back up at me, his eyes pleading.

"I don't want to die alone, Aurora," he says. "And I can tell I don't have much time. I just want to know I'm going to be close to you again."

He reaches for me but I bat his hands away. I know what he wants, but I can't bring myself to do it. Not now. Not when he's so close to turning. I don't want to end up fucked up for the rest of my life, just like him.

"Please, Aurora," he whispers. "It feels like days since I've bitten that lip."

Not the lip!!

My lady parts start to warm up, despite the fact I'm sitting at a tiny tea party table with my nutty mother and a man who's on the express train to Zombieville.

"My home is quite large if you two young people would like some privacy upstairs," my mom says, gesturing at a grand staircase that doesn't exist. "I'll have the servants show you the way."

"No thanks, Mom," I tell her. "We're fine right here."

"I told you I'm not into necrophilia," I hiss at Caligula. "No more sex! You're cut off!"

"I'd love to see the house," Caligula says, lurching to his feet and grabbing my arm.

"Please, Aurora," he says, crushing me against his chest. "I just want you to hold me. I'm afraid."

He's pale and weak and, for the first time it feels like he's being completely honest with me. It's so uncharacteristic that I pause. He wraps his arms around me and our eyes lock. I think back to our first meeting when I tripped at his feet. How he helped me up from the floor and then helped me in so many other ways after that. Ways that felt odd or uncomfortable and even painful at times. Ways that felt incredibly good and wildly hot at others. Caligula has been my protector, my mentor, my suitor, my lover.

Now, if I'm not careful, he's about to be my undoing.

"Stay with me, Caligula," I tell him. "Fight it with everything you have."

"Just let me ... bite that lip ... one more time," he whispers, then collapses, bearing me to the floor.

Once again, I'm under him. *And not in a good way.*

"My goodness, you two are frisky, aren't you?" Mother prattles on, completely oblivious to the fact that Caligula has started to cough up blood. "I think I'd better excuse myself."

She totters off toward a hallway, and her caregiver moves aside, barely glancing up from her book. I look at the cover, wondering what the hell could be so engrossing. *Who would read a book about a gray silk tie?*

Caligula stops coughing, and his body begins to convulse. For a moment, it feels like he's humping me -- *just like old times!* -- then the convulsing suddenly stops, and he goes completely still.

Uh-oh.

I put my hands on his shoulders and push, trying to roll his dead weight off of me. But he's too heavy.

He's also moving.

Slowly, I watch as he raises his head. His eyes aren't the impossibly intense pools of green that I've come to know and love. Instead, they're gray, glassy and there's a lot more gunk in them than before. His skin is already starting to grow pale, as well. He opens his mouth, and a fetid stench hits me in the face like a slap.

"Braihhhhnssh," he moans, staring into my eyes.

Brains? Really? He's gone completely old school on me?

I rock to one side, then roll back the other way. He rolls with me, allowing me to reach into my back pocket and grab my gun. But before I can do anything with it, his arm slaps it out of my hand. It spins across the floor and comes to a rest near the dollhouse.

"Stop it! Stop it!" I shout, slapping at his face desperately. He seems puzzled, and it gives me enough time to grab a small plastic chair and shove it toward his head, legs first.

He rears back. I'm finally able to slip out from underneath him. He tosses the chair off to the side and lunges at me, but only gets a mouthful of my coat.

Leather is *the only way to go!* I finally realize.

I scramble across the floor toward the kitchen and pick up my gun, then take a breath and aim for his head. He's moving faster than I expected, though.

Apparently, all of his training has turned him into some kind of super zombie.

I start pulling the trigger, hoping for a head shot. Instead, I make eight neat holes in his torso. I'm instantly sprayed with blood from head to toe. I close my eyes, praying the spatter doesn't make it into my system. I step back, slipping a little in the blood. Caligula moves forward and starts to lose his balance, as well.

"Mrrrrrrgggggh."

"I'm going to assume that means 'put me down before I kill anyone,'" I say. "But I don't speak zombie."

I scan the room, trying to locate a weapon. The other patient is long gone; the caregiver as well, although she's left her book. I wonder briefly if I could somehow smash his skull in with the thing, then quickly dismiss the idea. *Too lightweight. I need something more substantial.*

Caligula is watching me from the other side of the room, blood from his wounds draining onto my mother's painting, obliterating the blues and greens. It had been a dog. Or maybe a house. Now it's a post-apocalyptic abstract.

Suddenly, he comes at me again. I start throwing whatever's within reach at him: the dollhouse, a plastic frying pan, a wooden banana, a naked doll. Nothing stops him. I pepper him with wooden blocks, magic markers, the S and T volumes from the 1989 World Book encyclopedia set, some toy cars.

He slips on the latter and falls. I hold my breath, hoping he's brained himself. But after a moment, he gets back up.

Just as in life, the man's unstoppable.

I head for a doorway and slip through, finding myself in a kitchen. I try for the knife drawer, but it's locked. There are some appliances on the counter: an electric mixer, a cast-iron waffle maker, a beat-up toaster. I grab the toaster by the cord and swing in slow circles, waiting for Caligula to burst through the door.

I don't wait long.

When he comes through, I let loose and hit him square in the face. But it's not enough. *I should have gone for the waffle maker.*

He pins me up against the counter and tries to take a bite of my shoulder, but my coat stops him again. With my free hand, I continue to pummel him with the toaster, my fingers in slots like I'm wearing a giant metal boxing glove. But it's no good. I need something heavier. Something sharper. Something more lethal.

"Jesus, why didn't I pay more attention to you when I had the chance?" I scream at him. "Why was I such an idiot? You weren't *that* good in bed, you know! Not good enough to die for!"

Caligula pauses at the sound of my voice and despite myself, I suddenly begin to blush.

"Well, okay, you were pretty great, but still not good enough to go through all of this," I tell him. "To lose my friends. My family. My life."

He's listening to my voice, I realize. Listening and acting as if he remembers something. I see his glassy eyes staring at my lip. I bite it.

It's a mistake. Caligula suddenly lunges at me, trying to bite it, too. It's all I can do to push him off of me and keep a few inches between our faces.

"Rsssosooooghhhh," he breathes and I try to convince myself he's not saying my name. His body is pressed against me, his mouth moving toward mine slowly, tantalizingly. *Even in death, the man is a total sensualist.*

I do the only thing I can without a free hand. I bite my lip harder. And then I bite off a chunk. Just as his mouth is about to touch mine, I spit it across the room. It splats against the wall, then slowly slides down like a small bloody snowball.

Caligula turns his head, his grip easing up on me.

"Slprrrr?"

I reach out my hand and grab the handle of the waffle iron.

"Mgrinnnnnnnee!" he says, lurching over to the bloody chunk of skin on the floor. He picks it up and is about to pop it in his mouth when I brain him.

I hit him once for Hoser and once for Pen and once for my poor addled mother. I hit him a dozen times for all the students who died trying to learn how to hunt and kill these wretched creatures. I hit him for Mr. Austin back at my old school and for the crazy guy in the elevator with the blow-up sex dolls. I hit him for our cock-eyed Space Needle and the sunken ferries out in Puget Sound and our once-beautiful city that's now a decimated wasteland. I hit him for all the times we'd flirted and fought and fucked and futzed with that stupid contract which didn't do squat to save the city like he promised. And then I hit him one more time because his own insanity brought him to this sad, pathetic end.

Pieces of his skull are everywhere by the time I stop pounding.

I've ruined his hair forever.

Tough titty, growls my inner girl with the dragon tattoo.

Spent, I stand and turn on the water in the kitchen sink. It's light brown and lukewarm and there's not much more than a trickle, but it does the job. I wash my hands and face. Suddenly, I smell the scent of lemon and disinfectant.

"I thought you might need this, Miss Foyle," Trafalgar says, handing me a thick white towel.

I bury my face in the towel, sobbing quietly. Try as I might, I still hear the sounds. The wet thunk of the waffle iron. The crack and split of his skull. And at the end, his final syllables, a rattling moan that could have been nothing. Or could have been the words, "I love you."

"Thankkghss, Trafahgalgrgar," I say, handing him the towel. How he'll get those blood stains out, I'll never know.

On the other hand, if I stick around the tower, I may just find out.

"Actually, the name's Joe," he says. "Green called all of us Trafalgar for some reason." He gives me a shy smile and for the first time I notice he's got green eyes.

I smile back -- as much as I can with part of my lower lip missing -- and wipe Caligula's final words from my brain as neatly as I cleaned the blood from my hands.

I'm not that crazy. At least not yet.

"Nithe to mheet you, Joe," I say, then go into the other room to gather my mother and whatever's left of her wits. It's time to take her home.

Thanks for reading!
-B F

Coming soon?

FIFTY SHADES BRAINIER

B F Dealeo

CPSIA information can be obtained at www.ICGtesting.com
Printed in the USA
LVOW10s1718240713

344448LV00013B/1291/P